STOLEN PASSIONS

Stolen Passions

Kay Cavendish

HEADLINE
Liaison

First published in 1996
by HEADLINE BOOK PUBLISHING

A HEADLINE LIAISON paperback

10 9 8 7 6 5 4 3 2 1

ISBN 0 7472 5245 9

Typeset by
Letterpart Limited, Reigate, Surrey

Printed and bound in Great Britain by
Cox & Wyman Ltd, Reading, Berks

HEADLINE BOOK PUBLISHING
A division of Hodder Headline PLC
338 Euston Road
London NW1 3BH

Stolen
Passions

One

Tracy sat on the rose pink velour sofa with her legs tucked comfortably underneath her, flicking desultorily from *Anne and Nick* to *Richard and Judy* on daytime TV. The length of the items shown on the programme matched her concentration span, but nothing caught her attention sufficiently to want to watch it from beginning to end. She felt restless, unable to settle to anything. On the coffee table beside her she had, strategically placed, an oversized mug of steaming, milky coffee and a box of continental chocolates, now half empty.

She yawned and stretched, rearranging her satin housecoat around her bare legs and reaching over for another chocolate as the news was announced. Tracy switched the television off via the remote control. She didn't like watching the news, it was always far too depressing. All those starving children and war-weary mothers – it wasn't as if she could *do* anything. That's what Andy always said, anyway. Why upset yourself when there's nothing you can do? Best not to know, not to think about things like that. He was right, of course. Andy was usually right.

Tracy leaned back on the sofa and closed her eyes. He

1

had been right last night when he had told her she would enjoy using the vibrator he had brought home for her. Tracy felt hot all over as she thought about it. It was made of latex, coloured bright pink, and it had felt surprisingly warm against her skin. Andy had stroked it softly against the side of her neck, making her shiver. Tracy traced its path now with her fingers, caressing herself, recalling her apprehension as her husband whispered soft, seductive words against her ear.

'You'll love it, baby – feel how big it is. Think how it will feel, moving against your skin . . . inside you . . .'

'No!' she had murmured, half appalled, half excited by the images he was creating in her mind.

'I'm going to rub it between your tits . . . over your nipples . . . let me switch it on.'

Turning the base, Andy had set the dildo vibrating softly against her cheek. Cleverly, he had waited until she was fully aroused before introducing the vibrator and Tracy had been unable to resist its seductive lure. Remembering now, in the cold light of morning, she reached into the voluminous pocket of her robe and her fingers closed around it. Why she had brought it downstairs with her, she didn't care to imagine. She only knew that replaying the scenes she and Andy had enacted the previous night was making her hot, desperate for another session with the latex monster.

Bringing it out of her pocket, Tracy rolled it against her cheek, keeping her eyes closed to seal her own private world of fantasy from the distractions of her workaday life. Behind her eyelids, she saw herself as she had been last night, legs splayed apart, hands gripping the iron bedstead above her head as Andy tormented her with the vibrator.

With it he had sought out every erogenous zone, some which she never even knew she had, playing the vibrating shaft across her skin.

Slowly, Tracy twisted the base of the dildo until it began to purr. Stroking it across her lips and down her throat, she slipped it inside the opening of her robe and allowed it to rest against one soft nipple. Instantly, the flesh puckered and hardened, cresting into a tumescent peak as the gentle vibrations tantalised every nerve ending.

Rolling the dildo across the front of her breasts, Tracy subjected the other nipple to the same treatment. She felt as though her nipples were connected by some invisible cord to her clitoris, for it immediately began to swell and pulse. Perhaps it was the memory of Andy bringing her to the brink of orgasm over and over again the night before, holding her off until, at last, he had turned the dildo to maximum and the vibrations had ripped through her with a violence that had taken her breath away. Or maybe it was simply the ability of the vibrator to cut through her usual requirement for extended foreplay and catapult her to the brink and beyond within minutes.

Now, as she half sat, half lay on the sofa in the living room of her neat, modern house, playing with her new sex toy, Tracy imagined that she was in a richly decorated boudoir, allowing herself to be used by a stranger while Andy watched. It was a fantasy that Andy himself had implanted in her head, an image of herself which had grown and taken shape over the months until it was Tracy's fantasy too.

She groaned softly as the pressure of the vibrator against her now rock-hard nipples became uncomfortable and she moved it lower, over her rib cage and down towards the soft swell of her belly. Impatient with the restriction of her robe, Tracy pulled at the belt, flinging the two halves of the robe aside so that it lay open, giving her easier access to her own body.

In her imagination, it was the stranger who was controlling the pulsing instrument, teasing and tantalising her with it. Exposed to him as well as to her husband, who would be watching her, Tracy writhed, unable to disguise the acceleration of her arousal.

The vibrator hummed monotonously as she allowed it to rest on the sparse, crinkled hair of her mons. She could feel the referred ripples of pleasure travelling down towards her vulva. Using her other hand, she played with her breasts, kneading and squeezing the pliable flesh.

She was proud of her breasts. They were large and firm, topped by over-sized areolae the colour of ripe cherries. Pressed together, a deep channel was formed between them, perfect for the rhythmic slip and slide of Andy's penis. He liked to oil her breasts before fucking them. Now they were made slippery by sweat and Tracy brought the vibrator back up, twisting it round so that the rounded head was pointing towards her face.

Turning it up, she captured it between her breasts by pressing their sides together with her hands. Looking down, she could see the head of the mock penis poking out from between her breasts. It was vibrating wildly, making the flesh surrounding it shiver and shake.

If she spent enough time on her breasts, Tracy knew they were sensitive enough to make her come without her even touching the melting place between her legs. But she didn't want that, not this time. Now, alone with her fantasies, she had no patience for a leisurely climb to orgasm. The need had been building in her stealthily since she woke up that morning.

Allowing the dildo to slip out from between her breasts, Tracy took control of it again and pressed it deliberately against the hard little button of her clitoris. Pushing the vibrator into her body had made Andy so excited that he had come there and then, shooting his sperm all over her stomach and thighs. And afterwards he had been so loving, so good to her . . .

Tracy cried out as the first waves of orgasm washed over her. The cinematic pictures playing across the insides of her closed eyelids became faster, chasing one another across her vision until they became blurred into one amorphous impression of lust. Herself writhing in the throes of climax; Andy jetting his sperm over the whiteness of her skin; a dozen faceless men pleasuring her with hands and tongues and cocks, making her quiver and scream.

Bucking her hips, Tracy reared up off the sofa, slamming back down again on the soft cushions and scissoring her legs in the air, trapping the dildo between the swollen folds of her labia.

'Oh-oh-oh!' she cried, curling herself into a ball and rocking back and forth, her eyes tightly closed. Every nerve ending seemed to buzz along with the vibrator and she sighed as it dropped from between her legs and rolled on to the rug below, where it lay, humming softly, its noise muffled by the carpet.

Through the crack in Tracy's half-open door, a figure

watched, motionless, as she masturbated with the dildo. It was apparent from the way she abandoned herself that she was completely oblivious to everything but the clamorous needs of her own body. What would she think if she knew she was not, after all, alone in the house?

The intruder shivered at the idea of being seen, of the woman's reaction when she discovered she was being watched in her most intimate moments. It was an intrusion far more personal than mere robbery, and the figure in the doorway savoured the idea of it.

It was tempting to open the door, to go across and join the woman on the sofa. How would she react? Would she scream and fight? Or would she be so aroused she would regard the unexpected presence of another merely as an extension of her fantasy? Perhaps she would not pull away if another hand closed over the end of the vibrator? Maybe she would simply part her legs and submit, glad of the company . . .

The intruder moved away, jaw set as the distracting images continued to thwart the true purpose of the visit. Stealthily creeping up the stairs, he located the master bedroom with unerring accuracy. That was the plan, not the indulging of fantasy. The sight just witnessed was a bonus, all the more delicious for the fact that the woman had not known she was being watched.

Relishing the memory, the burglar went to work.

The sound of ringing woke Tracy with a start. Lifting her head from the cushions, she groped groggily for the telephone and lifted the receiver.

'Hello?'

'Tracy? Is that you darling?'

'Yes.' Tracy hauled herself to a sitting position as she recognised the sultry tones of Sheila, her neighbour.

'You sound half asleep! I was ringing to see if you'd like to join me for an afternoon drink, say, in half an hour?'

'Oh – right. Yes, that would be lovely. See you soon.'

Replacing the receiver, Tracy struggled to emerge from the fog of sleep. Vaguely, she was aware of a quiet buzzing sound that didn't quite belong in the living room. By her feet she saw the pink vibrator half buried in the pile of the rug and bent down to switch it off. Glancing at the clock she saw that it was twelve-thirty – she must have been asleep for the best part of an hour.

Tracy blushed as she thought of how she had spent her morning. Somehow she couldn't imagine the other women on Holly Lane being quite so self indulgent. Especially not Sheila, in her immaculate, antique-filled living room. The very idea of it made her smile.

If she was to visit Sheila for drinks, she'd better hurry and make herself look presentable. Getting dressed would be a good start. Tracy shuddered to think what her mother would say if she could see her swanning around in her dressing gown in the middle of the day!

The trouble was, she had so little to do, she mused as she wandered up the stairs. She and Andy made very little mess, so the housework was easily taken care of, leaving the rest of the day stretching before her, with only the preparation of their evening meal still to do.

Tracy sighed. She'd have to talk to Andy again about going back to work, if only part time. Giving up when they married had seemed like the sensible thing when she had thought herself to be pregnant, but now . . . now she had to have something to fill her day.

It wasn't as if there was anyone around in Holly Lane during the daytime anyway, apart from Sheila. All the other women worked, except for Lulu, of course, but then she had her work cut out looking after JD. At seventy-four Lulu's husband was not as fit as he had been when Lulu married him two years before. Caring for him qualified as a full time job on its own.

Going into the bedroom, Tracy stopped in her tracks.

'Oh my God!' she breathed.

When she had left the bedroom that morning, it had looked immaculate. Tracy never allowed herself to go downstairs until the bed looked as she wanted it to look when it was time to get back in again. Now the pristine white, *broderie anglaise* trimmed duvet cover was crumpled and besmirched with what looked like muddy footprints. The contents of her chest of drawers and her dressing table were strewn around the room and her jewellery box had been turned upside down in the middle of the bed, her jewellery lying in a jumbled heap beneath it.

'Oh no!'

Tracy scrambled feverishly through the tangled chains and baubles, realising at once that everything of real value – her engagement ring, her grandmother's pearl earrings and the necklace Andy had bought her on her wedding day, to name but three – had gone.

How could someone have broken into the house and ransacked her bedroom while she was still at home? The thought of it made Tracy's skin crawl. Then she remembered what she had been doing before she fell asleep on the sofa and her breath caught in her chest.

Tracy sank onto the bed, her legs turning to jelly as she imagined what could have happened if the intruder had caught her *in flagrante* with the vibrator. It was bad enough to know her privacy had been violated thus far, that some-one had been in her bedroom, rifling through her jewellery and her drawers.

Her eyes fell on the mess of clothes lying in disarray on the floor by the bed. She felt sick as she realised that it was mostly underwear that had been turned over. What kind of pervert had been in here? Whoever it was, they must have been delighted to find her collection of crotchless panties and peephole bras and other mildly kinky undies that Andy regularly brought home for her.

Tracy closed her eyes as she dwelt on it. She would die if anyone found out what she wore during the most intimate moments of her relationship with Andy. And, if she was any judge, so would Andy himself.

Her hand trembled as she reached for the telephone extension by the bed. The large car dealership where Andy worked as a senior salesman was always busy and it took the receptionist several minutes to locate him. When he finally came on the line, he sounded impatient.

'Tracy? What's wrong?'

'Andy— I—' to her horror, Tracy started to cry.

'What is it? Tracy – are you ill?' He sounded more impatient than concerned and Tracy made a gargantuan effort to pull herself together.

'No . . . can you come home?' she managed to gulp.

'Now? For God's sake, Trace! You'd better tell me what's happened.'

9

'We've been robbed.'

There was a stunned silence on the other end of the telephone.

'Robbed?' Andy echoed. 'But you said you were going to stay home all day today—'

'I have!' she interrupted him. 'Oh, Andy, please come home! I'll explain everything then.'

'All right . . . calm down, Tracy. Look, it might take me a while to get back. Why don't you call Sheila to come and sit with you until I get there?'

'No! I don't need a babysitter, Andy. I just want you.' Aware that she was beginning to whine, Tracy forced herself to ring off. Remembering that she was supposed to be at Sheila's for drinks, Tracy punched in her number.

'Sheila? It's Tracy. I know, I should have been with you by now, but . . . something's happened. I'm afraid I won't be able to make it.'

She explained, briefly, about the robbery and endured Sheila's well-meant outrage.

'Have you called the police?' the older woman asked her.

Tracy had to admit, her first thought had been to telephone Andy. She always relied on him to know what to do – it wouldn't have occurred to her to phone the local police first.

'I'll wait for Andy to come home,' she told Sheila now, 'he'll report it, I expect.'

Sheila made an impatient sound at the back of her throat at Tracy's timidity, though when she spoke again her voice was kind.

'Well, don't touch anything, Tracy. You don't want to disturb any clues, or whatever it is they'll be looking for.

Will you be all right on your own?'

'Yes thank you. I'll see you soon.'

'Right. Let me know all the details though, will you? We can alert the neighbours at our next Neighbourhood Watch meeting, on Friday. You haven't forgotten, have you?' Sheila said when Tracy did not respond. 'Friday night here at Rose Cottage? Rob is so looking forward to it – I think he's got rather a special film for us all to watch when the business part of the proceedings is concluded.'

Tracy felt her stomach muscles clench as she thought about the Neighbourhood Watch group. Last month they had spent precisely half an hour on the 'business part', as Sheila called it, before commencing what, to most of the people gathered, was the real reason for their meeting.

The first time she and Andy had attended a Neighbourhood Watch meeting Tracy had been shocked at the casual exchange of partners. She had heard of wife swapping of course, but she had never really believed that it actually went on. Or that she could enjoy it as much as she did. One thing was for certain: it would throw them all to have a real crime to discuss.

'Tracy?'

'Yes, sorry, Sheila, I was miles away. Of course we'll be there on Friday, both of us. I have to go now. 'Bye.'

Once she'd put the phone down on Sheila, Tracy found she could not bear to leave the mess, so she set to, tidying up. The police were hardly going to pull out all the stops for such a small robbery, she reasoned, and it was going to have to be done in the end anyway.

It was as she was sorting through her undies that she realised that several items were missing. A black lace teddy with suspenders attached which she had put in the drawer only that morning, a particularly garish red PVC-look body and a black push-up bra that gave her a cleavage to die for.

Somehow the idea that someone had stolen her under-wear was even more distressing than losing her jewellery. The jewellery had sentimental value, to be sure, but the fact that it was the sexiest items of underwear that had gone missing made it more personal somehow. The idea that the thief had gone through her knicker drawer and selected the items he would take made Tracy feel quite ill.

Forcing herself downstairs, Tracy made herself a hot drink and went back into the living room to wait for Andy.

Andy drove home in a top of the range, low-slung sports car, one of the showroom's demonstration models. This was a perk of the job that he thoroughly enjoyed and he had to resist the temptation to take the beauty on to the dual carriageway for a quick spin.

Tracy had sounded quite frantic when she telephoned, but then his wife always sounded quite frantic. Andy sup-pressed a sigh, trying not to allow the crushing feeling descend that he always felt when he thought about his wife. If there hadn't been that pregnancy scare, he knew they would never have got as far as marriage. It hadn't really crossed his mind to leave her holding the baby, so to speak, as many of his mates had urged. He wanted to do the right thing by her.

A phantom pregnancy. He thought that was the kind of thing that only happened to heroines in Victorian novels, not to modern young women in the nineteen-nineties. But that was what Tracy had had. A phantom fucking pregnancy.

So here he was, Andy Davis, senior sales director for Ashford Motors, well on the way up the ladder, a house on Holly Lane and a bimbo for a wife. Andy instantly felt guilty. Tracy wasn't a bimbo, not exactly. She was just so . . . *needy*. She looked to Andy for his opinion on everything, from what she should wear to whom she should invite in for coffee.

At nineteen Tracy was a good six years younger than he, so he supposed it was natural that she should look up to him to some extent. And the sex was good – they had no problems in that department whatsoever, he thought, remembering the fun they had had together the night before.

Even so, Andy reflected as he pulled into the tree-lined thoroughfare which led to Holly Lane, what he really wanted was a partner in life, a true equal. Someone like Sheila Blake, he said to himself as he pulled into Holly Lane and saw Rose Cottage on the corner.

He smiled to himself as he always did at the name, a misnomer if ever there was one. Rose Cottage was more like a manor house than a cottage. And Sheila was very definitely the lady of the manor, mistress of all she surveyed.

Andy felt a thrill as he pulled into his own driveway. Sheila could be mistress over him any day. She was the reason why he went to the monthly Neighbourhood Watch meetings, for Andy lived in hope that one day he might find himself paired with her. In her early forties, Sheila was in her prime. She had the kind of look in her eye that spoke of self assurance and Andy was convinced that she would display the same aplomb behind the bedroom door that she employed in her everyday life.

He envied Rob, Sheila's husband. How liberating it must be to be relieved of the constant responsibility, the expectation that he would take control of each and every situation. If only Tracy could be the same, if only once. Cutting the engine, Andy sat in the car for a moment and allowed himself to indulge in his favourite fantasy: of Sheila, dressed in the black rubber catsuit he had once seen her wear, enticing him to her room and proceeding to ravish him, stripping him of every last vestige of control over his own body.

'Andy! Andy!'

He was snapped out of his pleasant daydreams by his wife calling to him from the doorway. She was in her dressing gown and her pretty face was anxious as she waited for him to get out of the car. Smothering a sigh, Andy pinned a reassuring expression on his face and went to gather her into his arms.

'Oh, Andy!' Tracy breathed in the familiar scent of him as he enclosed her in his embrace. She felt so relieved that he had arrived. For the past hour she had tormented herself with such imaginings and she realised that she had actually worked herself into quite a state.

'Come on – show me what's been happening.'

They walked up the stairs together and Tracy showed him her ransacked jewellery box and her disturbed underwear.

'There are some things missing,' she said, 'things from my chest of drawers.'

'What things?' Andy asked her patiently, sensing from

her tone that there was more to this than met the eye.

Tracy swallowed, averting her eyes as she told him.

'Shit! You mean some pervert has stolen your underwear?'

Tracy nodded and Andy realised that she was very close to tears.

'Come on,' he said soothingly, anxious to avoid a watery scene, 'don't upset yourself.'

Tracy allowed herself to be comforted and led out of the room.

'I'm sorry,' she said, 'it's just the thought of someone rifling through my things . . . it makes me feel dirty.'

Looking up, she saw that Andy had steered her into the spare bedroom. Closing the door behind them, he took off his jacket and loosened his tie. Tracy's jaw dropped. How could he even think of sex at a time like this?

'Andy – I don't think—'

'Ssh!' he silenced her with one finger against her lips. 'I know what you need, baby. You're so tense . . . I know how to relax you.'

If Tracy hadn't spent time playing with the vibrator she might have responded more eagerly, but now she shook her head emphatically.

'No, Andy, I—'

'What's this?'

She groaned with her eyes as Andy's fingers closed round the dildo in her pocket. Dammit, she had forgotten it was there! When she opened them again Andy was watching her with a knowing smile playing around his lips.

'What have you been doing with this, Baby?' he asked her, his voice dropping an octave as it always did when he was aroused.

'Nothing,' Tracy replied, embarrassed to admit that she had been masturbating while he was out at work.

'Nothing?' Andy grinned. The idea of her using the vibrator on herself obviously excited him.

'Don't you think we ought to phone the police about the break-in?' Tracy suggested feebly as he reached into her robe and cupped one naked breast in his hand.

'That can wait,' he whispered, his lips against her hair and his thumb brushing rhythmically back and forth across her nipple. 'I can think of far more interesting things to do with the rest of the afternoon, can't you?'

Tracy felt the familiar spreading warmth of desire and she nodded.

'Mm. But Andy—'

'No buts,' he interrupted her. Lowering her down onto the spare bed he covered her upper body with his, his lips roving her hairline, her neck and the swell of her breasts at the opening of her robe.

Tracy shivered and tangled her fingers in his thick crop of chestnut brown hair. She loved it when he made an unexpected pass at her like this, wanting sex when she least anticipated it, demonstrating time and again how easy it was for him to draw a response from her body. She was like putty in his hands, she mused dreamily as he pulled the two sides of her robe apart and nuzzled the warm cleft between her generous breasts. Andy knew exactly which buttons to press, which words would drive her wild with desire so that everything else was chased out of her head.

Now she moaned softly as Andy's lips moved lower, lingering on the soft swell of her belly, brushing along the crease where her pubic hair began.

'I can tell how aroused you've been,' he told her, raising his head to see her reaction. 'You're so warm and sticky . . .'

He slipped his first two fingers into the folds of her vulva, parting the sensitive lips and stroking the silky slick channels of flesh. Tracy moaned softly, her sleeping sex flesh responding instantly to his touch, swelling and moistening, opening to him like a flower in the sun.

'That's it, baby,' Andy whispered, his voice husky with excitement, 'give it to me.'

He dipped his head and replaced his fingers with his tongue, exploring each tender fold as if sampling the most exquisite of desserts. Tracy felt her clitoris harden and press forward, eager for the flick of his tongue. Andy did not disappoint her. Teasing the area around it with the very tip of his tongue, he waited until Tracy was writhing with pleasure before catching the little bud between his lips.

'Ooh!' she cried, spreading her legs wide and pushing her pelvis forward as he worried at it with his lips, triggering wave after wave of pleasure. Everything slipped from her mind except the rising tide of the desire which now swamped her. Her breath came in rapid little gasps, her heart hammered frantically in her chest and her stomach muscles clenched as her sex flesh convulsed in the throes of orgasm.

Within minutes, Andy had pushed down his trousers and had slipped inside her, in time to feel the pulsing of the internal walls of her vagina gripping him, bringing him quickly to a climax himself.

Tracy was unable to swallow a whimper as Andy pulled out of her as soon as he had come.

'Don't go back to work yet,' she pleaded, sure he was able to turn around and leave her.

Andy gave her an incredulous look.

'We need to phone the police, Trace, or had you forgotten?' She flushed at the knowing look in his eyes.

'Only momentarily,' she said defensively.

Andy smiled, though not unkindly, and held out a hand to help her up.

'I was right though, wasn't I, baby? I knew exactly how to calm you down.'

'You're always right, Andy,' Tracy replied through clenched teeth.

She didn't like his attitude just lately, she mused as she walked over to the window. Sometimes Andy came a little too close to her liking to saying that he could read her like a book. She had no illusions about his feelings towards her; theirs was hardly a marriage made in Heaven. And, it was true, she did like sex, very much. It was the thing that they most had in common. But she resented Andy's implication that he could control her with it.

'You'd better get dressed,' he told her now. 'I'll make the phone call.'

He joined her at the window and, as if sensing that he might have overstepped the mark, he slipped his arms around her waist, resting his chin on the top of her head.

The window of the spare bedroom, like their own, over-looked the cul de sac. As they watched, a removal van drew up outside the house next door, closely followed by a couple in a dark blue saloon car.

'That'll be our new neighbours,' Tracy said. 'I wonder what they're like?'

18

Andy did not reply. Like Tracy, he was watching the couple who had parked their car on their new driveway with interest. The man, slightly older than himself, he guessed, was passably good looking with blond hair and a fresh face, but he had the beginnings of a beer belly, just showing above the waistband of his jeans. He looked a pleasant enough chap, though unremarkable. It was the woman who really caught Andy's interest.

She was dressed, like her husband, in jeans and a plain shirt, though unlike him there appeared to be not an ounce of spare flesh on her. Her medium length fair hair was pulled back into a ponytail and she looked anxious as the removal men began to unpack their furniture.

'She looks nice,' Tracy said, a shade wistfully, Andy thought.

'Hmm. There's something about her, though . . . I wouldn't have thought they were very well suited.'

Tracy looked over her shoulder at him in surprise.

'Whatever makes you say that? How can you tell just by looking at them?'

Andy felt uncomfortable. He wasn't generally thought of as a particularly perceptive man, nor would he want to be. Now he felt embarrassed for thinking aloud.

'I don't know,' he replied with an uncharacteristically self deprecating shrug. 'Body language, I suppose.'

As they watched, the man went up to the woman and looked as though he would kiss her on the cheek. The woman, however, rather skilfully avoided him, pretending not to notice that he had approached her.

Tracy glanced at Andy.

'Maybe you're right,' she conceded. 'Anyway, it's none of

our business. I just thought she might be someone I could get to know. It gets lonely stuck in the house all day on my own.'

'Why don't you go over and introduce yourself later, after the police have been?' Andy suggested, losing interest in their new neighbours. 'You could suggest they attend Friday's Neighbourhood Watch meeting – get to know the other people on the street.'

He grinned wickedly and Tracy looked away from him, back to the woman next door. She looked like the sort of woman who would be shocked to the core by what went on amongst the residents of Holly Lane.

'Maybe,' she replied distantly. *Or maybe the new neighbour would simply be a friend*, she added silently as Andy went downstairs. Goodness knew, she needed one of those.

Two

Alice Grainger glanced up at the bedroom windows of the house next door and saw the woman watching them. She hesitated, unsure whether to wave, or to pretend she hadn't noticed. The decision was taken out of her hands when the woman, realising that she had been seen, moved away.

The woman at the window looked very young, Alice mused as she directed the safe delivery of her three-piece suite into the living room. She hoped that she was friendly. It would be nice if she could make a friend; leaving her neighbours in their last street had been the hardest thing about moving here. In truth, if she had had her way, they would never have moved at all, for she had been happy enough in their cosy little semi. It was Des who wanted them to 'better' themselves by moving here.

Alice watched her husband now, busily unpacking a tea chest, and she felt the all too familiar wave of exasperation and affection for him. He was as excited as a child before Christmas, preening over his new acquisition. If only she truly loved him, then maybe she would be able to share his sense of achievement. After all, it was Des's hard work which had enabled them to buy this house. Alice hadn't worked since she was made redundant twelve months before.

She sighed now. It was no good, starting off in a negative frame of mind. She had made her decision, knowing that it wouldn't be easy – now she had to stick to it. It wasn't as if she actively disliked Des, indeed, they rubbed along quite nicely together. There were far worse marriages which were supposedly based on love.

Agreeing to their move to Holly Lane had been Alice's way of showing that she was prepared to make a go of their marriage, that she wanted it to work.

Feeling guilty now for the way she had avoided his kiss earlier, Alice went over to Des and gave him a quick hug.

'I'm going inside to find the kettle and a couple of mugs – I think we deserve a drink, don't you?'

Des grinned.

'Yeah – but not of tea! C'mon, Alice, where's your sense of occasion? There's a bottle of bubbly in the coolbag. It's been in the fridge all night.'

Alice opened her mouth to protest. After all, it was only two o'clock in the afternoon. Instead she forced a smile.

'That'd be lovely – see you in the kitchen in a minute then?'

Des nodded, watching her until she disappeared inside. Alice hadn't wanted to move, he knew that, but she seemed to be quite happy today. Her pale skin was flushed underneath its smattering of pale freckles and her eyes seemed bright and excited. Maybe things were going to be all right after all.

Alice found the bottle of champagne and, though it was still quite cool, put it inside the pristine new fridge that had come with the house. She had to admit, it was a lovely kitchen. All gleaming white surfaces on top of rag rolled, eggshell blue doors.

Wandering through to the living room, she saw Des tipping the removal men before they climbed into the van and drove away. The previous occupants had left their soft piled cream carpet and Alice gave in to the instinct to kick off her shoes and curl her bare toes into the carpet. It felt soft under her feet as Alice paced the room from one corner to another, getting the feel of the place.

Their furniture: a three-piece suite; bookcase; china display cabinet and nest of coffee tables, had been pushed into a jumble in one corner of the room, leaving the rest of it feeling bare and echoey. Wandering back to the kitchen, Alice met Des as he came through the front door.

'Well, this is it!' he said, beaming from ear to ear. 'Home sweet home!' He rubbed his hands together with undisguised glee and gave Alice a hug. She had to smile at the sheer little boy enthusiasm. 'Where's that champagne?' he asked.

'In the fridge.'

Des made an impatient noise in the back of his throat.

'It must be cold enough by now – come on, help me find some glasses.'

They'd unpacked half the crockery before they came to the glassware, by which time Alice felt she would far rather have a cup of tea. They hadn't eaten since breakfast and her stomach was beginning to make its disapproval known, rumbling and complaining as she straightened. Wisely, she kept her thoughts to herself and returned Des's grin as he uncorked the champagne and poured the frothy liquid into her glass.

'Here's to a new home,' he toasted her, clinking his glass against hers, 'and to us,' he added, his voice low and smoky.

Alice felt a moment's panic which she quickly suffocated. She wouldn't let any doubts resurface to spoil this moment for Des.

'To us,' she echoed, before tipping up her glass and downing its contents, far too quickly.

Inevitably, the bubbles surged up her nose and made her hiccup. She laughed and Des refilled her glass. His sense of achievement at moving into number two, Holly Lane, was almost palpable.

'I can't believe we're really here,' he said now, shaking his head in wonder. 'When I was a kid I always knew I'd end up in more than a two-up, two-down, but this—' he made an expansive gesture with his arm '—I never dreamt I could get this far.'

'*We* could get this far,' Alice corrected him gently, filling her glass for the third time. She could get to like this champagne drinking lark, she thought as it took the edge off her hunger. It wasn't as if it was that alcoholic, she told herself; she couldn't feel any effect whatsoever even after three glasses. And it tasted divine.

'Of course. I couldn't have done it without you, sweet-heart.' Des put his arm round her and, for once, Alice didn't automatically shrink away. In fact, she felt quite affection-ate towards him, quite warm.

He was stroking her arm now through the thin cotton of her sleeve and Alice found she liked the gentle caress. Perhaps the champagne was not quite as harmless as she had first thought, she acknowledged, for the kitchen seemed to have taken on a rosy glow and cotton wool to have wound its way round the inside of her skull.

Leaning her head against Des's shoulder, she sighed contentedly.

'I think we'll be happier living here, don't you?' she said dreamily.

Des picked up the champagne bottle and emptied it into Alice's glass.

'I hope so,' he said, his voice dark and husky.

Alice drank her bubbly, aware of the tension transmitting itself from Des's body to hers. The softness of her breast was pressed against the hard wall of his rib cage and she felt herself respond to his closeness as she hadn't responded in quite some time.

'Des?' she said, not daring to look directly at him.

'Mmm?'

'Do you think . . . all that marriage counselling, the sex therapy . . .'

'Yes?' he prompted when her voice trailed away.

Alice gave a small, uncertain smile. Putting her glass on the counter – carefully, since the surface seemed to be undulating gently before her eyes – she looked up at him. He was watching her warily, his grey eyes darkening as he saw what was going through her mind.

'I think I might be drunk,' she told him with a little laugh.

Des smiled.

'I think you might,' he agreed, reaching out to tuck a stray frond of hair behind her ear.

It was a small gesture, but its tenderness made Alice's breath catch in her throat, affecting her far more than any blatant pass would have done. If she tried, she could come up with any number of reasons, good reasons, why she should turn away, start unpacking or whatever and pretend that she had not noticed the onset of the lengthening tension between them. But that had been her trouble all along, she recognised now – she thought things through too much, so that by the time she had sorted out her feelings the time for action was past.

Taking a deep breath now, she said, 'I was wondering . . . do you think we could . . .? I mean . . . could we?'

She couldn't quite bring herself to say the words, though she was aware that her body language was talking for her. Leaning towards Des, the tips of her breasts brushed provocatively against his arm and her lips parted and trembled.

'Do I think we could what?' Des asked her, an amused smile playing around the corners of his mouth.

Alice felt herself grow pink. It wasn't like her to take the initiative like this and Des wasn't making it easy for her. The champagne might have lessened her inhibitions, but she was sober enough to know that what she was suggesting represented a huge step forward in the rebuilding of their relationship.

Des must have realised this too, for, taking pity on her, he tipped up her chin between his thumb and forefinger and kissed her, oh so gently, on the lips.

Alice moaned and swayed against him, wanting him to deepen the kiss, yet afraid to make the move herself. She couldn't remember a time when she had felt more aroused, more in tune with her body than she did at that moment.

She shivered as Des ran the tip of his tongue along the tender skin on the inside of her lower lip. Pressing her against the kitchen worktop, he explored the sensitive recesses of her mouth with his tongue, coaxing her tongue to parry with his, resting his hands on the slender curve of her waist.

Below the softness of his belly, Alice could feel the hardening shaft of his penis through the thick denim of his jeans as his pelvis pressed against hers. Usually this crude evidence of his arousal was enough to dampen what little ardour he managed to provoke, but this time, for some inexplicable reason, she found herself returning the pressure boldly.

He was still a little afraid of rushing her, for he pulled away, his eyes searching hers for an instant, before dipping his head and burying his lips in her hair.

'Oh Alice!' he breathed, his voice ragged and wondering, as if he couldn't quite believe the change in her.

Alice pressed her palms against the broad expanse of his back, stroking him as his lips kissed a path from her neck round to her ear. She gasped as he caught the lobe between his teeth and nibbled gently. It was as if there was a small electrical charge running from her earlobe through to her breasts and down, to the very core of her. The tender, secret folds of flesh between her thighs fluttered and swelled as she allowed sensation to subvert reason.

Perhaps it was the champagne, allowing her to close her mind to rational thought and concentrate fully on the sensations overwhelming her. Goodness knew, she only understood at that moment that what she was doing with Des felt good and, for some reason, what she *felt* was far more important to her at this moment than what she *thought*.

She clung to him as his lips moved lower, tracing the shape of the neckline of her blouse, teasing the firm upward curve of her breast. Alice felt that every part of her was supersensitive, as if each inch of skin was affected by the slightest stimulation of the inch next to it, so that sensation flowed through her body in a ripple effect, causing her to tremble at the sheer enormity of it.

Gradually, she began to respond less passively: tangling her fingers in Des's hair, pressing her own lips against his forehead and grinding her hips against his. Des broke away for long enough to look down at her with overbright eyes. Alice saw the desire written clearly in them and felt a little rush of pleasure that she was the cause of it.

'Let's christen the new house,' he suggested breathlessly.

Alice frowned, unsure what he meant and he smiled at her, his lips travelling across her face, lingering against her mouth.

'Let's make love in every room,' he said, his breath brushing softly over her lips.

'*Every* room?' she echoed, her voice no more than a seductive whisper.

'Mmm. I want today to be a day we remember all our lives.'

His mouth covered hers, drawing a response from her, and Alice allowed herself to lean into him, moving without protest as he manoeuvred her through the kitchen door and into the living room. A giggle caught in Alice's throat as she felt the soft pile of the carpet beneath her bare feet again and she imagined herself lying naked on it, while Des stroked her skin.

A part of her mind, the part that was still rational, remembered that there were no curtains at the window and the afternoon sunshine was streaming through the glass. She thought of the woman next door, watching them as they unpacked and shivered.

'Des – the window . . .' she muttered between kisses.

He glanced over at it and shook his head.

'It's too high for anyone to be able to see in. Besides, we're set back from the road. Relax . . . forget it . . .'

Alice didn't need any further encouragement. She helped Des to unfasten the tiny buttons of her blouse, shuddering as his lips touched the gentle curve of her breast. Kneeling at her feet, he slipped the buttons of her jeans through the stiff buttonholes and pushed them down, over her hips, so that she was left in nothing but her plain white cotton panties and matching bra.

'Oh Alice!' Des said with a catch in his voice as he stood back and looked at her.

Alice recognised the admiration in his eyes and felt an atavistic tingling deep in her womb. It wasn't very often that she stood so unselfconsciously semi-naked in front of her husband and yet she found she liked the feeling which trickled through her when his eyes lingered.

She still felt a little muzzy headed, but she knew that in fact she no longer needed the excuse that she had drunk too much to make love with Des. It had helped, initially, to break down her inhibitions, but now Alice was conscious that she didn't need to hide behind it any more.

All those months of sex therapy and all it had taken was a few glasses of champagne on an empty stomach and in the middle of the day! Her mouth curved upwards.

'What are you laughing at?' Des asked her, smiling as he took her into his arms.

Alice told him and he laughed with her, but not for long. Pulling off his shirt, he stepped close to Alice. She could feel the heat emanating from his body, drawing her closer until her breasts were flattened against the hair-roughened planes of his chest. She felt a moment's panic as his hands cupped her cotton-covered breasts, gathering them up and squeezing.

'Gently,' she said, panic colouring her voice. 'Please . . . take it slowly.'

Des stroked the exposed skin on the upper curve of her breasts with his fingertips and smiled at her, understanding, it seemed, her need.

'Yes,' she murmured, her eyelids drooping as the exquisite feathers of sensation tickled through her, 'yes, that's right.'

Des eased her a little to her right, so that she was standing in a pool of sunlight spilling through the window.

'You look like an angel,' he whispered.

Pulling the band out of her ponytail, he ran his fingers through her long, fair hair, spreading it like a shawl around her shoulders. Alice shivered, feeling the goosebumps rise on her skin as Des continued the gentle stroking. Reaching out, she traced the line of his neck down to his collarbones, smoothing her fingertips along them until they met in the centre.

Des moaned softly and leaned towards her. Dipping her head, Alice retraced the path her fingers had taken with her lips, ending up at the point where his collarbones met. His skin was warm and slightly salty. Dabbing at the dip at the bottom of his throat with the tip of her tongue, Alice tasted the sweet saltiness of his skin and traced a damp line up to the protuberance of his adam's apple.

His hands came about her waist, smoothing and stroking the skin so lightly that Alice imagined she could feel each tiny hair standing on end. She felt tense, afraid, still, that Des would become impatient and rush her, bring things to a conclusion before she was ready. But he seemed to sense that they were on the verge of something special, that to rush her now would be to destroy something that so far hadn't had time to blossom and grow.

His hands had worked round to the back of her now, and Alice gasped as she felt the catch to her bra give. It fell to the floor soundlessly and Alice felt the very tips of her nipples graze against the coarse hair on Des's chest. The small stimulation sent a crackle of sensation through her, transmitting itself to her burgeoning sex flesh which moistened and swelled.

Alice was having trouble breathing, her whole body seemed to quiver and shake. Des held her firm, his lips seeking out the warm dip of her neck, his palm polishing the roundness of her shoulder. Her breasts were crushed against him, yet she could feel the tips, like two hard, round buttons, distinct from the soft, pliable flesh surrounding them.

Des's fingers worked their way under the elastic of her panties, the middle finger of one hand finding the bony promontory of the base of her spine. Alice sighed as he rubbed at it, feeling the strange pressure deep inside the cradle of her pelvis. Slowly, Des drew her panties down over her thighs. Sinking to his knees on the soft carpet, he dragged them down to her ankles, then he lifted each of her feet in turn and removed her panties completely.

Alice stood stark naked in the middle of their new living room, gazing down at her husband's head as he bent to kiss her feet. The whole scenario felt surreal. She felt disconnected from her body, as if she was outside herself, watching what was going on with wide eyes. Waiting for the next act.

Des's lips were moving over her toes, kissing each one, his tongue dipping into the groove between. Alice stood very, very still, concentrating all her attention on the tiny patch of skin which Des was pleasuring at that moment. Closing her eyes, the room faded from her consciousness, place and time slipping out of focus, fading in importance.

She felt weightless, her body fluid as Des began to kiss a path up her legs, transferring from one to the other and back again, so that no part of her was untouched by fingers or lips. There was a fluttering in her belly, a trembling as he neared the joining of her thighs. Alice knew that she was wet, the physical evidence of her arousal coating the swollen, tender leaves of flesh still hidden from his view.

'Oh!' she whispered as his hands came up, cupping her buttocks and stroking them, his fingers digging slightly into her flesh. *Please let him carry on like this*, she said fervently in her head, *please don't let him lose patience!*

Alice gasped aloud as Des knelt up and pressed his lips against the soft swell of her stomach. His mouth slipped against the silky surface of her skin, sending shivers up her spine. Covering her breasts with her own hands, she circled her palms over the sensitive tips, activating a chain reaction from her breasts to her vulva.

Des was now nuzzling the light fuzz of pubic hair which covered her mound, his tongue probing at the beginning of the cleft of her vulva. Barely aware of what she was doing, Alice moved her feet apart, feeling her labia peeling away from each other, exposing her inner skin to Des's exploring tongue.

The first touch of his tongue against her clitoris sent a minor explosion of pleasure along her nerve endings, curling into a knot in her belly. Alice pinched her nipples between fingers and thumbs, tweaking them as he made his tongue into a point and wriggled it along the channels of flesh between her legs.

God, it felt good! Alice allowed her head to fall back on her shoulders as Des entered her with his tongue. The silky, pleated walls of her vagina convulsed around it, her clitoris pulsing against his fingertips as he circled it. Her hair fell down the centre of her back in a soft, ticklish curtain, her breasts thrusting upwards, eager for the firm touch of her fingertips against the nipples.

Oblivious now to everything except the growing clamour within her body, Alice bent her knees, bearing down on to Des's mouth, pushing her clitoris out so that it butted against his nose. She was coming; she could feel it building up, growing inexorably stronger, until she could no longer hold it back.

Reaching down, she meshed her fingers into the hair at the sides of Des's head, holding him still as she circled her hips, grinding her pelvis against his upturned face, masturbating against him as her orgasm broke.

'Jesus, Alice! I thought you were going to suffocate me!' he gasped as they fell to one side, Alice exhausted, sated by him.

Slowly, she opened her eyes. He was looking at her as if he didn't know her, his pupils dilated, his mouth open, taking in air. An image of herself, out of control, using Des to bring herself to the peak, pushed its way rudely into the post coital fog which enclosed her, and she flushed.

'I'm sorry,' she whispered.

Des's eyes widened.

'Sorry? Jesus, Alice, don't be sorry! Be grateful . . .' he added, rolling towards her and picking up her hand, 'by all means be grateful . . .'

He guided her hand to his crotch and closed it over the hardness of his shaft still contained by the denim of his jeans. Alice felt the heat of his erection and felt her heart sink. Of course, there had to be payback, a price for her pleasure.

Des would want like for like – fellatio in exchange for the satisfaction his tongue had afforded her. Alice imagined herself unbuttoning his fly, slipping his fat, firm penis out of his underpants and easing the foreskin back with her fingers. The end would be slippery, glistening with the clear fluid of pre-emission which she would surreptitiously wipe away with her thumbpad before bending her head and dabbing at the slit with her tongue . . .

'C'mon, sweetheart,' Des said, his voice thick, as if his tongue had swollen in his mouth, 'show me how grateful you are . . .'

Alice sat up reluctantly, allowing her hair to fall in a concealing curtain around her face, masking the distaste she knew would be obvious in her eyes. She hated this. More than anything she hated this. *So tell him*, a voice in her head told her, *offer him something else instead.*

Looking up at Des, her hand still on the bulge in his jeans, Alice saw that his eyes were shining, almost glazed with anticipation. Again she imagined her lips stretching over the shiny head of his cock, drawing it in, sucking at it until the fluid leaked into her mouth, slippery and warm . . . she almost gagged even as she thought about it.

Becoming impatient with waiting, Des began to unbutton his jeans himself. Alice felt herself begin to shake. She couldn't do it, she couldn't . . .

Gathering her courage, she opened her mouth to tell him so, when she realised there was someone tapping on their front door. Des heard the sound at the same time and they looked at each other in horror.

'Quick – you get it while I get dressed!' she whispered, already gathering up her discarded clothing. Supposing whoever it was stepped on to the front garden and looked through the living room window when they didn't answer the door? Supposing they already had?

'Oh God!' she groaned, fumbling with the catch to her bra. 'Stall them, Des – I won't be a minute!'

Des buttoned up his shirt and, with a glance at Alice to see how far she had got, closed the living room door behind him. As she fastened her jeans and blouse and pulled her hair into a rough ponytail, Alice heard his voice in the hallway, accompanied by another, definitely female one. She heard Des laugh and marvelled at his ability to sound so normal. For her part she was sure that anyone would need only to glance at her to guess that she had recently been in the throes of ecstasy, and she was rigid with embarrassment even before the living room door opened and Des showed their visitor through.

It was their neighbour, the woman whom Alice had seen watching them from the upstairs of the house next door. She was wearing a fluffy, short-sleeved, pink jumper and a white skirt which ended just above her knee. Her legs were bare and brown, shown to advantage in the high-heeled white sandals.

'This is Tracy,' Des was saying, 'Tracy, this is my wife, Alice.'

'How do you do?' Alice said formally, her own awkwardness making her sound prim and unfriendly.

'Very well thank you,' Tracy replied, smiling warmly at her.

Tracy had the kind of girlish, breathy voice which would make it difficult for anybody listening to her to take what she was saying seriously. Alice wondered whether this was an affectation, or a genuine impediment.

'Here – why don't we all sit down,' Des said, extracting the sofa and chairs from the mélange of furniture dumped by the removals men in the corner of the room.

Alice smiled at Tracy, more warmly when she considered how she had saved her from having to perform oral sex. If only her new neighbour knew! She smiled to herself. Anyone would think she had been saved from a fate worse than death!

'I'll make some tea,' shall I?' Des said as the two women sat at either end of the sofa.

'Thank you,' Tracy replied in her little girl voice, 'that would be lovely.'

The two women watched him leave. Once they were alone, Tracy turned to Alice and regarded her with what Alice thought was a speculative gleam in her eye.

'I just called by to welcome you to Holly Lane,' she said formally, 'and to invite you to join the Neighbourhood Watch group.'

'Neighbourhood Watch?' Alice frowned. 'I'm surprised you need one round here.'

Tracy laughed humourlessly.

'Oh, you'd be surprised!' she said. 'Only today we were burgled next door!'

'No! How dreadful for you! Did they take much?'

Tracy's eyes slid away from Alice's as she replied in an unconcerned tone which sounded remarkably false.

'Not much. Just some jewellery and . . . some clothes.'

'Clothes?'

'Yes.' Tracy smiled brightly. 'Anyway, don't let me alarm you on your first day here! I just thought you might like to come on Friday, to Rose Cottage – you know, the big house at the beginning of the Lane? Sheila and Rob are hosting the meeting this month. We usually have a . . . a get together afterwards, so you could get to know all the neighbours.'

Alice beamed. It sounded like the quickest way of getting to know people in their new home and she readily accepted the invitation.

'Do I need to go to Rose Cottage beforehand and introduce myself to the hostess?' she asked.

Tracy shook her head.

'No need – you'll have enough to do between now and then, what with unpacking and finding your way around. Are you local?'

'No, we've moved from Tilbury.'

Tracy's smile brightened.

'Well, maybe you'd like me to show you around. I'm in all

day, so any time that suits you would be fine by me.'

Returning her new neighbour's smile, Alice accepted the offer. Her smile extended to Des as he came in with a trayful of tea things and his eyebrows rose, though he looked pleased to see Alice happy.

'Tracy's offered to show me round the neighbourhood,' she explained as he joined them.

'That's great.' Des smiled warmly at their new neighbour. 'It'll make things so much easier for Alice if she has someone to talk to sometimes while I'm out at work.'

Tracy gave him a smile, then turned her full attention on Alice.

'It'll be good for me too,' she said warmly. 'I have a feeling that you and I are going to be great friends.'

Impulsively, Alice leaned forward and squeezed Tracy's hand.

'Me too,' she said. 'Great friends.'

Three

Across the street, in the upstairs bedroom of number five, JD McFarlane watched the small exchange between the two women with a little pang of excitement. He had liked the look of the new girl from the moment he saw her from behind the net curtains of his bedroom.

Now seventy-four, JD had been a woman-watcher all his adult life. He prided himself on being able to sum up a girl's sexual personality within five minutes of meeting her. He'd had plenty of experience – married five times, his fifth (and, he guessed, final) wife had been a mere slip of a girl of nineteen when he married her. Such was JD's charm, Lulu had fallen in love with him despite his dratted impotence, and showed every sign of still adoring him two years on.

Now he put down his binoculars and smiled thoughtfully. He had always liked young Tracy from number one. She was a bit scatty, but she had a heart of gold and he didn't like to see the way that young scallywag of a husband treated her. No matter how strong a man's basic drives, there was no excuse for humiliating one's wife. There were ways, after all, to make a woman feel loved and cherished, as a woman should. Making her feel insecure, battering at

39

her self esteem was reprehensible. Unforgiveable.

As for this new woman – well! JD suspected repression, and repression – or, at least, the curing of it – was something that was guaranteed to warm the cockles of an old man's heart!

He turned as he heard the bedroom door open, smiling as Lulu walked through. Even after three years his heart flipped over like a young, lovesick calf every time he saw her.

'You're looking very lovely, my dear,' he said now. 'That shade of blue really suits you.'

And indeed it did, he told himself, holding both hands out to her. The all in one trouser suit she was wearing – a flying suit they would have called it in his younger days – was made of silk with a smooth finish which made it glow dully in the electric light. The deep, sapphire blue brought out the unusual colour of her eyes, eyes which were sparkling now as she took his hands and twisted to the left and right, pretending to pose for him.

'What have you been up to?' she asked him, eyeing the binoculars on the windowsill.

JD smiled and drew her into the circle of his arm.

'Our new neighbour,' he told her, nodding towards the house directly opposite. 'They've been celebrating their move in the living room.' Thinking of the woman, her long hair streaming down her naked back, her neck arched as the man knelt between her legs made JD shiver anew.

Lulu's eyes lit up with interest.

'Really?' She peered closer and JD guessed she'd forgotten to put her contact lenses in again. 'Isn't that Tracy in there with them?'

'Yes. She arrived right in the middle of the action.'

'No! How did they react?'

'With horror, embarrassment, I would guess. I've never seen two people dress so quickly!'

Lulu laughed.

'We'd better stand back from the window – we don't want them to know they were being watched.'

'No one can see through these curtains, Lulu,' JD explained patiently, knowing she didn't trust them.

It wasn't that Lulu would mind other people watching her; she had an exhibitionistic streak which made her the perfect mate for JD. But she also had an honourable distaste of watching people who didn't know they were being watched, and while she was indulgent of JD's voyeurism, she refused to take part in it herself unless the participants were fully aware and agreeable.

'I wonder if Tracy's invited them to the Watch meeting on Friday?' she said as she pulled her husband away from the window.

'Hmm. It might be a bit too soon . . . still, we'll see, won't we?'

'Could be interesting.'

'New blood.'

They smiled at each other, in perfect accord. Lulu grimaced suddenly.

'I almost forgot why I'd come up to find you! Sonja's called round for a coffee – would you like to come down and join us?'

JD's eyes lit up at the mention of their next door neighbour.

'Sonja? We haven't seen her for a week or two.'

'No. Apparently Liz has been a bit difficult.'

'Ah.' Liz, Sonja's partner, was like a disapproving parent at Watch meetings and she certainly did not approve of Sonja's forays into the sensual world of the house next door.

'Where is Liz now?' JD asked as he followed Lulu slowly down the stairs.

'On the allotment apparently. Don't worry, darling – you're perfectly safe!'

JD gave a weak smile. He made no secret of the fact that he was terrified of Liz. She never bothered to hide her contempt, she clearly thought he was a dirty old man. Well, perhaps he was, he thought defiantly to himself. Lulu didn't mind. It wasn't as if he was out prowling the streets or anything like that; Lulu made sure everything was kept under control. However, he wouldn't put it past Liz to burst into their kitchen like a Fury to drag Sonja back home, and the idea of that made JD break out in a sweat. He didn't like that kind of unpleasantness, it wasn't good for him at his time of life.

Sonja smiled as they walked into the kitchen.

'I thought you two had got lost!' she said goodnaturedly.

JD went over and kissed her on both cheeks.

'You have to forgive an old man,' he told her, sitting down in the chair that Lulu had pulled out for him. 'I'm slow, but I always get there in the end! How are you?'

Sonja shrugged her shoulders and her smooth auburn hair swung softly around her delicately made face.

'Bearing up, you know?'

'Liz still giving you trouble?' JD enquired sympathetically, smiling his thanks at Lulu who had passed him a coffee.

'A little.' Sonja sighed and her fingers fluttered in a gesture of resignation. 'Liz wants fidelity, she simply can't accept the way I am. Especially my liking for the odd cock.'

JD's eyebrows rose and he roared with laughter as he was caught unawares by Sonja's unexpected crudity.

'Shame on you – such language coming from such lovely lips!' he said in mock reproof.

'Ooh yes – such lovely lips!' Lulu echoed, leaning over Sonja's shoulder and fastening her mouth on hers.

JD watched as the two women kissed, openmouthed and hungry, tongues thrusting and duelling before they broke apart, suddenly. Both were flushed and Sonja's beautiful green eyes had darkened to a stormy emerald.

'More coffee anyone?' Lulu asked innocently, but JD noticed there was a slight crack in her voice which betrayed her mood.

He smiled to himself as he picked up his coffee cup. His wife was in the mood to play, and when Lulu wanted to play . . . catching Sonja's eye across the wide, old fashioned pine table, he raised his coffee cup to her in a silent toast and winked.

Liz dug the spade savagely into the soil and turned it over before repeating the process. She was sweating in the afternoon autumn sun, her vest grubby and stained, her cotton trousers and wellingtons caked in mud. Damn the torrential rain that had waterlogged her plot and damn Sonja for skiving off and leaving her to do the chores on her own – again.

Glancing over at the McFarlane's house, the garden of which backed onto the allotments, she scowled at the windows. They seemed to glare blankly back at her and she renewed her efforts with the spade.

She knew where Sonja had gone. A sharp stab of something like pain prodded her and she was appalled to feel unwanted tears welling in her eyes. It wasn't as if she was afraid that Sonja preferred that fluffy bimbo at number five. Sonja loved Liz, she only amused herself with the others. Liz understood that, but she couldn't seem to inure herself to the hurt of it.

Dammit, wasn't she enough? Didn't she give Sonja everything? Liz couldn't see why Sonja felt the need to make love with Lulu, especially not with that old lecher, the Colonel, watching.

Liz's lip curled as she thought of JD. Impotent old goat! She'd seen him, spying on everyone in the Lane with his binoculars. Well, she'd better not ever catch him spying on her and Sonja, or she'd ram his binoculars somewhere so uncomfortable that he'd never be tempted to lift them to his eyes again!

Straightening, Liz suddenly had the curious feeling that she was being watched. She frowned, turning her head towards her own house, number four. Eyes narrowed, she scanned the upper windows, but there was no one there.

Of course there's no one there, you fool, she chastised herself roundly as she turned away and carried on with her digging. There were only two people who lived at number four Holly Lane – herself and Sonja. She was here, working her fingers to the bone to get the vegetable patch in order, and Sonja was . . . Sonja was cheating on her with that promiscuous bitch next door.

Thinking of JD and his binoculars had made her para-
noid. There was no one watching her. No one cared what
she did anyway. Shrugging her shoulders, Liz put her back
into her work and shut her mind off to anything else.

From the upstairs window of number four, a figure watched
Liz work. For a moment there, the intruder thought that
Liz had seen a movement at the window, but she had clearly
dismissed the idea. The intruder smiled. How easy it was to
remain undetected.

The back garden of number four was almost entirely
devoted to self sufficiency. Rows of vegetables and live-
stock, in the shape of a few hens and a milk-yielding goat,
dominated the space, making the small flower bed in the
corner look incongruous. Liz had installed a gate in the
fence to make it easier to get from the garden to the allotment. Her tools were propped up beside it now, in easy
reach. A hoe, a digging fork and a wheelbarrow, stacked
with bags of fertiliser. It would be heavy to manoeuvre
through the small gap.

It was hard work watching Liz digging – she was relentless, driven. The intruder smiled again. No doubt it was the
thought of Sonja having 'coffee' next door that was driving
her!

Come to think of it, now might have been a good time to
do number five. Normally the old boy was a menace with
his binoculars and his tireless snooping, but if he was
otherwise engaged . . . Concentrate! One job at a time.

Opening the drawers, the intruder was disappointed to
find nothing but practical, utilitarian underwear, nothing
of any real interest at all. Nothing much was expected from

Liz, but Sonja was a disappointment. Thinking of the naughty, sexy bits and pieces acquired from Tracy's drawers earlier made the disappointment more acute. But then, there had been more than one bonus at number one, so it was hardly very fair to compare number four unfavourably. Smiling at the memory of Tracy with her vibrator, the intruder pocketed several pairs of plain white pants and a pair of bright blue bedsocks anyway, before looking round for more valuable spoils.

There was very little jewellery, which was disappointing, but there was a very pretty little ormolu clock on the bedside table that looked as if it might be valuable. And cash. Around £500, at a rough count, rolled and kept together with an elastic band, shoved carelessly into the bedside drawer. That would do nicely.

Deciding that there was nothing more to be had, the intruder slipped away, unseen.

In the kitchen of number five, JD helped himself to a cherry and sultana cookie and watched as Lulu assembled the ingredients for the fruit flan she had promised him for dessert later. He thought it odd that she had decided to continue with her cooking when Sonja had come for coffee and there were far more exciting pursuits on offer, but he didn't comment, preferring to sit back and listen to the two women talking.

'Are you and Liz going to the Watch meeting on Friday?' Lulu asked as she floured the marble board which she had placed in the centre of the table around which they all sat.

'*I'll* be there,' Sonja replied, her eyes, like JD's, following the quick movements of Lulu's hands as she kneaded the pastry.

'What about Liz?'

Sonja shrugged.

'I don't know. She's not that keen and it kind of holds me back a bit, if you know what I mean.'

Lulu smiled.

'Does she know you're here now?'

Sonja looked uncomfortable.

'I don't know. Probably. I—' she trailed off with a frown, her teeth worrying at her lower lip.

'What is it?' Lulu prompted gently.

Sonja shook her head and laughed, a short, nervous sound that had Lulu and JD exchanging puzzled glances.

'Nothing. I've been a bit worried about Liz just lately, that's all.'

'In what way?' Lulu persisted.

Sonja shrugged again.

'I don't know. She's been behaving a bit . . . well, oddly, I suppose. Not like herself at all.' Once again, she gave that short, nervous laugh, only this time she waved away her own concern with the fingers of one hand. 'Ignore me, it's nothing, I'm sure.'

'Well, I suppose if there is something bothering Liz, she'll tell you eventually. Won't she?'

Sonja smiled weakly.

'Probably. What's that you're making?'

Taking the hint, Lulu allowed the direction of the conversation to be changed.

'Fruit flan. It's JD's favourite.'

Sonja saw the affectionate smile that passed between

husband and wife and felt a pang of envy. Despite the very obvious differences between them, Lulu and JD seemed so happy together. If only she and Liz were so easy with each other, maybe there'd be a chance that they could work things out between them. But they weren't: Liz was too possessive and she was too fickle for either of them to be really happy in anything but a fleeting affair.

It had been a mistake to move in with Liz, Sonja knew that now. In truth, she had to admit that she had realised her mistake very quickly once Liz had explained her version of the good life to her. All that digging and planting and environmental concern – Sonja couldn't see what was wrong with picking up a ready meal in the supermarket, never mind growing the ingredients in the back garden!

Still, she had been in love then, and Liz's passionate beliefs had seemed like an endearing quirk. It was only recently that she had found it all so irritating, and that was hardly Liz's fault. After all, it wasn't Liz who had changed, it was Sonja herself, and Sonja's feelings for Liz. And very soon the time was going to come when she would have to do something about them.

'Sorry?' She started as she realised that JD had said something to her.

'I was asking you if you cook,' the old man explained patiently. 'Lulu is a wizard at it.'

Sonja looked across the table to where Lulu was now peeling grapes and arranging them in the shortcrust pastry case she had made. There was flour on her forearms and hands still and the juice from the grapes had formed blurred runnels through the flour coating her skin.

'No, I don't cook,' she replied absently, her eyes on Lulu's fingers as she began to peel a satsuma. 'At least, not if I can help it.'

'Pity.' JD sounded disappointed as he sat back in his chair.

Lulu caught Sonja's eye and smiled at her.

'I doubt if you get much time anyway, commuting every day,' she said.

'Modern women!' JD cut in, in a tone of mock despair.

Lulu and Sonja both laughed. As Lulu arranged the segments of orange in the flan case alongside the grapes, she suddenly held out one to Sonja.

'Would you like some?'

Sonja looked from her to the orange segment and back again. Lulu's deep blue eyes were bright, looking straight through her, her gaze steady. Sonja's lips curved upward in a small smile.

'I thought you'd never offer,' she said, her voice husky.

Holding Lulu's eyes, she leaned forward and took the segment between her teeth. As she bit into it, the sweet juice spurted down her throat and she swallowed. Watching her, Lulu picked half a grape out of the flan case and held it out to her. Again, Sonja took it between her teeth, only this time she drew Lulu's fingers into her mouth with the fruit.

JD expelled his breath on a blissful sigh, but both women ignored him as Sonja sucked the fruit juice from Lulu's fingers. With her other hand, Lulu selected a ripe cherry from the small pile of fruit she had ready to peel. Pressing it against Sonja's teeth, she applied enough pressure for the fruit to burst, sending the juice dripping down Sonja's chin.

The two women rose in unison, leaning across the table to kiss. Lulu licked the sticky cherry juice from Sonja's skin before nibbling at her lower lip with her teeth. Sonja's lips parted, allowing Lulu's tongue access to the inner recesses of her mouth. Lulu could taste the fruit juices still clinging to her tongue and the sides of her cheeks.

'Mmm – you taste so-o good!' she murmured as they broke apart.

Sonja's cheeks were flushed, her eyes bright as she regarded Lulu across the table. Her fingers hovered at the neckline of her button front T-shirt, as if she wasn't quite sure if it would be in order for her to undress.

'Let me help you with that,' Lulu said softly, solving the dilemma for her.

She undressed her quickly, stripping away her T-shirt to reveal her small, unfettered breasts, then easing her jeans and panties down over her hips together. Sonja was very slender, fine boned with no surplus flesh to soften the lines of her body. Her pubic hair was a deep, dark red, but sparse, carefully groomed to perfection.

JD took all this in in a single glance. He had seen Sonja naked before, of course, but that didn't diminish his pleasure at looking at her now. Glancing at his wife, he saw that Lulu was as entranced as he. Her eyes flickered in his direction and he smiled at her, signalling his pride in her.

Sonja was standing very, very still, waiting. Lulu smiled at her, reaching across the table to take her hand. Holding her hand, she walked around the table so that she was standing in front of her.

'Why don't you lie down, Sonja?' she suggested in her soft, musical voice. 'This table is surprisingly strong – isn't it JD?'

'Oh yes,' he replied, his voice thick with suppressed

excitement, 'very strong. They don't build them like this any more.'

As if hypnotised, Sonja turned and, sliding her bottom on to the edge of the table, she lay down slowly, on her back. Reaching out, JD fingered the soft fall of her hair as it splayed across the table.

'Beautiful,' he whispered, almost to himself, 'like silk.'

Lulu smiled indulgently at him.

'Keep your hands to yourself, JD – wait until you're invited!'

Stripping off the all-in-one trouser suit she was wearing, Lulu revealed that she was naked underneath. JD grinned. Lord, how he loved this woman! Always ready for an adventure, always dressed – or undressed – ready for action!

The tension between the two women was palpable as Lulu climbed on to the table and, gently nudging Sonja's legs apart, placed one knee between them, the other to one side. Reaching across to her selection of fruit, she made a show of choosing the ripest strawberries which she carefully de-cored before putting one between her teeth.

JD watched as she put her hands on either side of Sonja's head, and slowly lowered her face to hers. Sonja's full, red tinted lips parted as Lulu transferred the strawberry from her mouth to Sonja's. As Sonja ate the strawberry, Lulu dabbed at the corners of her mouth with her tongue, catching any dribbles of juice which escaped whilst at the same time driving Sonja wild with desire.

Picking two more strawberries, she rolled them gently on the very tips of Sonja's nipples. She had small breasts, so much so that when she was lying flat on her back, as now, her chest was virtually flat. Her nipples, though, were long and responsive, almost as red as the strawberries.

Sonja gasped as Lulu applied enough pressure to crush the berries against the rubbery flesh of her nipples. The juice ran down her breasts, the pulp forming a messy film on her teats. JD licked his lips, but held himself back. He knew that, eventually, he would be invited to join in. He had only to be patient – and to savour the wait.

Lulu closed her mouth over one breast and sucked hard on the strawberry coated nipple. Sonja groaned and shifted her hips slightly, widening her legs. JD debated whether to move further down the table, so that he could see her sex displayed so invitingly, but then he would not be able to watch Sonja's face while Lulu was licking and sucking at her breasts, and that was a treat he was loth to forfeit. Sonja was incandescent with desire, her attractive face transformed to beauty by the strength of her emotions.

'Mmm – yummy!' Lulu said once she had cleaned all the strawberry juice from the other girl's skin. 'Now, let me see – what shall we have next? Ah yes – peaches . . .'

Sonja drew in her breath as she watched Lulu peel the velvety skin from the fruit. She trembled with anticipation, closing her eyes momentarily as she imagined what Lulu intended to do with it.

'Oh!' she cried out in surprise as, holding the peeled peach high above Sonja's stomach, Lulu squeezed it in her fist and the juice sprayed over her belly, pooling in her navel and running down into her pubic hair.

'Nice?' Lulu asked solicitously.

'Sticky.'

Lulu laughed, dipping her head to sip the juice from her

navel before reaching over to the fruit and picking up another peach.

'Here, JD – if you peel this for me you can have the pleasure of squeezing it. That's all right with you, isn't it, Sonja?'

Sonja nodded. Sex with Lulu always involved JD, that much was expected. By inviting herself in for coffee, Sonja had knowingly entered into an unspoken contract with which Lulu ensured that her husband, despite his inability to achieve an erection, would never feel left out.

Lulu smiled at her now and began to peel a small banana. Sonja watched her fingers, so soft and sensual, as they denuded the fruit of its skin. Soon those same fingers would be running over her own skin. The thought of it made Sonja shiver.

'Cold, my dear?' JD asked, noticing the small shudder.

'No, no I'm fine.'

JD nodded understandingly.

'Good. I wonder if you'd be so kind as to open your legs a little wider . . . that's right. Now, if you could just bend your knees up a little . . .'

Sonja moaned as she felt the wet flesh of the peach in JD's hand make contact with the heated, slippery folds of her labia. The moan was gagged by the gentle insinuation of the peeled banana between her teeth. Lulu was smiling as she closed her own lips over the other end of the banana and began to eat her way towards Sonja's mouth. Sonja copied her, chewing the end of the fruit and feeling it slip down her throat before the next part pressed insistently against her teeth.

Meanwhile, between her legs, she felt JD grinding the

peach into her sex, his bony fingers pushing the pulp deep inside the channel of her vagina, smearing the juices all around her vulva. From the corner of her eye, she saw him pick up a can of aerosol cream from the table and squirt it all over her open sex. Then, taking his chair to the end of the table, he held her thighs apart and dived in.

Lulu's lips met Sonja's and she began to lick the inside of her mouth, eating the banana which had slipped inside it. Sonja felt as if she was being consumed at both ends, as if both husband and wife were devouring her, using her as a channel for their mutual pleasure. JD's tongue was swirling around the entrance to her body now, teasing her inner lips apart whilst every now and again entering her with its tip, just enough to make her want more.

'Please . . .' she mouthed against Lulu's lips.

The other woman's breasts were hanging down and she brought up her hands so that she could fondle them. They were large and firm, the nipples smooth and hard beneath her palms. Sonja pulled gently at the teats and Lulu moved slightly, so that she could take one into her mouth.

As JD lapped at the now sticky folds of her vulva, Sonja suckled Lulu's breast. She felt JD move his attention to the sensitive skin surrounding her clitoris and she sucked harder, making Lulu gasp.

'Oh yes!' she breathed as Sonja grazed her swollen nipple with her teeth, 'harder – bite it . . . ahh!'

Sonja barely knew what she was doing, she was suffused by a wave of pleasure that made her feel hot from the top of her head to the tips of her toes. JD's teeth were worrying at the hard bud of her clitoris while Lulu's fingers tweaked almost painfully at her elongated teats. She nibbled on

Lulu's nipple, increasing the pressure as the other woman groaned.

JD seemed to have caught her clitoris between his teeth and was pulling at it, sending shockwaves of pleasure-pain through to her womb. It came, like a storm, making her buck her hips and cry out, releasing Lulu's nipple as she moved her head from side to side. JD lashed his tongue very quickly against the quivering bundle of nerve endings, prolonging Sonja's orgasm until she couldn't bear it any longer and she begged him to stop.

'Please JD, please, please . . . no more!'

Lulu climbed off the table and the two women looked towards JD. He emerged from between Sonja's legs with a beatific smile on his still handsome face. His chin was smeared with cream and peach juice, mingled with the secretions of Sonja's body.

'Fruit flan,' he said to no one in particular, 'my favourite!'

Lulu reached across Sonja and picked up another peach.

'Good,' she said, piercing the skin with her thumbnail, 'then you'll be up to having seconds . . .' and holding JD's eye, she spread her own legs apart.

Four

Liz regarded the patch of ground she had worked with a critical eye. It was no good, there was simply nothing else to be done with it. Her arms and legs were aching, she was filthy, her stomach grumbled with hunger and the light was beginning to fade. And still there was no sign of Sonja emerging from next door.

Feeling thoroughly fed up, Liz stacked her tools in the wheelbarrow and trudged home. Leaving her mudcaked wellies by the back door, she washed her hands in the kitchen sink, staring out into the back garden morosely.

She had planned to cook a vegetable bake for tea, but she was too bone weary to even think about it. Perhaps she'd feel better after a good soak in the bath. By the time she came out, Sonja would no doubt be home. She might even start the supper for her.

Upstairs in the bathroom, Liz stripped off her dirty clothes and dropped them in the washing basket. The small room filled with the scent of lilacs as the bath water frothed. Washing her short hair quickly in the sink, Liz wrapped it in a fresh towel and climbed into the bath.

Bliss! The water was hot and deep and the sweet smell of

the flower-scented bubble bath that her grandmother had sent her for her birthday lifted her spirits a little. Closing her eyes, she lay back in the water and let it soothe her aching muscles.

After a few minutes, her thoughts wandered, inevitably, to Sonja. There could be a perfectly innocent reason for her increasingly frequent visits to the house next door, she told herself. It could be that she really was only being neighbourly, as she claimed. It had taken Liz a long time to accept that Sonja didn't – couldn't – share all her interests, that she needed the company of other people.

For her part, Liz was more than content to live the life of a happy hermit, with only Sonja for company. She knew she couldn't force Sonja to feel the same way, and she was acutely aware that, the more she tried, the further Sonja pulled away from her, but she couldn't seem to help herself.

Liz couldn't rid herself of the notion that they were heading for a confrontation of some sort, and she was dreading it. The idea of losing Sonja made her feel sick. Yet, she had to admit, there was another part of her which wanted only for the uncertainty to end.

Tiring of her own thoughts, she stood up and covered herself with a homemade exfoliating cream. Using a large loofah, she rubbed at her skin until it glowed, taking pleasure in the way it made her tingle all over. After a quick sluice down, she stepped out of the bath and dried herself briskly before slathering herself in body lotion, again from a batch she had made up herself.

There were fresh jeans in the cupboard which she pulled out together with a lightweight, apple green cotton jumper. Pulling her underwear drawer open, Liz frowned. She liked to keep her panties and so on in nice, orderly little rolls. She liked order; it made her feel secure. The contents of her drawer were, however, very far from tidy. It looked as though someone had rifled through them, without regard for neatness or order at all.

Sonja? Liz dismissed the idea the minute she thought it. If by some chance Sonja had wanted to borrow something, she would have taken it without disturbing the rest of the contents of the drawer.

Frowning, Liz pulled on clean undies, then her jeans and sweater. It came back to her then, how she had felt as if she was being watched earlier, while she was in the allotment.

'Oh no – the money,' she whispered, rushing to the bedside cabinet and pulling open the drawer.

There was a glaringly empty space where the roll of money had been. Frantically, Liz pulled out the drawer and tipped it up. It was no good, the money she had been saving for Sonja's birthday had most definitely gone. She reached for the telephone.

Once she had been promised that there would be a policeman on her doorstep during the evening, Liz hung up the telephone and found herself at a loss. She could go and get Sonja, she supposed, but she still had some pride and was not willing to sacrifice it. The supper still needed cooking, but Liz didn't think she could face that either.

Remembering that the pub round the corner, on the main road had recently introduced a vegetarian menu, Liz made a snap decision to take herself out to eat. It was obvious that the local police did not regard her break-in, if indeed that is what it was, as a top priority – there was sure to be time to snatch a bite to eat before they came. Besides, Liz was overwhelmed by an uncharacteristic desire for company, and it was this that eventually drove her out of the house.

The Dog and Duck was a popular pub amongst the locals, so Liz wasn't surprised to see Sheila Blake from Rose Cottage, on the corner of Holly Lane, sitting on one of the high stools by the bar. They weren't particularly friends – the two of them had so little in common that friendship was virtually impossible – and Liz's first thought was to go into the bar before Sheila spotted her. Though she was pleasant enough, Sheila always knew everyone's business in Holly Lane, and Liz wasn't sure if she was up to listening to an update on all the neighbours' doings.

It was too late. Sheila waved at her across the room and beckoned her over. Liz smiled, though her heart sank. From the look on her face, Sheila had a juicy titbit of gossip she was dying to share, and there was no way of getting out of being the recipient.

'Hi Sheila,' she said, pulling out the bar stool next to her and easing herself on to it.

'Hello, Liz – we don't see you in here very often!' Sheila smiled warmly at her, opening up a fresh packet of cigarettes and lighting up.

'No, well, I didn't feel like cooking, so I thought I'd try the new menu here.'

'Of course, you're a veggie, aren't you? I've heard it's very good. Wouldn't do for me though, I'm afraid – I like my food like I like my men – oozing red blood cells!' She chuckled, taking a deep drag on her cigarette and tilting her head back so that the stream of smoke she blew out travelled over Liz's head.

Smiling faintly, Liz ordered a pint of lager and a stuffed aubergine with salad.

'I'm glad to have caught you actually,' Sheila said, having refused Liz's offer of another drink. 'Are you and Sonja coming to our place for the Watch meeting on Friday?'

At the mention of Sonja, Liz felt the heat seep into her cheeks and hoped it wasn't noticeable in the dim lighting in the pub.

'I think so,' she said noncommitally. 'What *is* that racket?' she said, turning in the direction of the hammering and drilling which had just started up outside.

Sheila grinned.

'Oh, darling, *that's* why I'm here.'

'Sorry?'

'I'm here to watch the new conservatory going up.'

Liz eyed her sceptically.

'Sounds about as exciting as watching paint dry,' she commented.

Sheila laughed.

'You're right. But I've got my eye on that young carpenter there . . . what do you think?'

Liz followed Sheila's gaze to where a muscular young man, stripped to the waist, was drilling holes in the wall. He had long, blond hair, tied back off his face with a spotted scarf and he didn't look any more than about eighteen.

'I would have thought he'd be a bit too young, even for you, Sheila,' she remarked, paying for her meal and taking her cutlery over to a table.

Sheila came to join her, since she would still have a good view of the patio outside. She didn't seem at all offended.

'They can never be too young, Liz. Just look at him – I bet he could keep it up all night.'

Sheila sounded wistful and Liz had to suppress a shudder.

'Sheila – you are incorrigible!'

'I know. But just look at him, Liz – even your mouth must water a little when you look at that bum.'

Liz shook her head and watched the youth walk across the patio to pick up another batch of nails. Personally, she simply couldn't see the appeal, although admittedly, from a purely aesthetic point of view, the young builder was rather beautiful. Sheila was right – he had a nice, tight arse under his grubby jeans and his upper body, though not overdeveloped, looked as though it could have been sculpted by Michaelangelo.

Giving herself a mental shake, Liz was brisk as she turned back to Sheila.

'Anyway – what was it you wanted me for? You said, when I came in, that you were glad to have caught me?'

'Oh yes.' Dragging her eyes away from the powerhouse of testosterone not thirty feet away from her, Sheila leaned forward and gave all her attention to Liz. 'Did you know that they had a break-in at number one this morning? Tracy lost some jewellery, from what I gather. She was quite upset . . . Liz? Darling, you look quite pale . . .'

'I . . . you took me by surprise, that was all. You see . . . we were burgled this afternoon while I was out on the allotment.'

'No!' Sheila was suitably outraged, but Liz could see a spark of excitement in the back of her eyes. She knew that look; it meant that she and Sonja would be yet another news item on Sheila's interminable grapevine.

'Yes. I'm expecting the police round this evening, in fact, so I'd better not linger over my meal.' She forced a smile for the girl who brought her her plate. She didn't feel nearly so hungry now and she began to pick at her meal with her fork.

'Why on earth didn't you say something when you first came in? I thought you looked a little strained but I thought it was probably to do with this business with Sonja and JD—'; she broke off suddenly as she caught the expression on Liz's face. It wasn't often that Sheila felt shamed by indiscretion, but she did now, and she turned her discomfort into a cough. 'Did they take much?'

'Just some money. I don't know if anything of Sonja's is missing . . .' Liz trailed off, knowing that if Sheila already knew there was something going on between Sonja and the McFarlanes she probably knew that Sonja wasn't at home. No doubt the rest of the Lane knew too. Liz half expected Sheila to offer some kind of hamfisted commiseration, but for once the older woman let sleeping dogs lie.

'Tracy sounded devastated – you must be feeling pretty shaky yourself?'

'I am a bit, actually. It's the thought of it, you see, of some bloke creeping around in your house, rifling through your things . . .' She bit her lip as she thought of the way her underwear had been disturbed. 'Bloody men!'

Sheila put a heavily ringed hand over hers.

'It's not necessarily a man, darling.'

'Yes it is!' Liz pushed her plate away, the meal barely touched. 'Another woman would know what it would feel like to be violated like this!'

'Calm down, Liz,' Sheila said gently.

Liz took several deep breaths, then smiled weakly.

'Sorry. I'm overtired and it's been a bad day – I think I'll get back. I ought to go really anyway, in case the police decide to come earlier than they said.' *And Sonja might be home by now*, she added silently to herself.

'I'll see you on Friday then?' Sheila said as she stood up.

'I expect so. After all, we've got some real, genuine Neighbourhood Watch stuff to discuss this time, haven't we?'

Thoughtfully, Sheila watched her go. Poor Liz, she'd been having a rough time of things lately. Lately? Sheila grimaced to herself. The way Liz chose to live must make life difficult for her at times in any event.

'Was there something wrong with the meal?'

Sheila looked up in surprise as the young girl who had served Liz dinner came to take her plate away.

'No, darling, nothing at all. My friend hadn't worked up enough of an appetite to do it justice, that's all.'

Turning her attention to the patio outside, she caught the young man she fancied staring at her and she smiled. He looked away quickly, a flush staining his cheeks. Sheila felt a thrill travel up her spine. God, she loved it when they were shy! He glanced up at her again through the glass, quickly, as if he was afraid that she would notice.

After a few minutes, Sheila got up and walked casually through the half open door into the garden. The young man was working a little apart from his work mates and she sensed him stiffen as she approached.

'That's a lovely piece of workmanship,' she said, running her fingers caressingly over the piece of wood he had just positioned.

'Thanks,' he mumbled in reply.

Close to, Sheila could see the smoothness of his skin beneath the light covering of stubble and she saw that he was, indeed, very young. As if he was unnerved by her presence, he straightened and looked quizzically at her. Sheila caught a waft of sweat and felt quite faint. The young man hooked his thumbs into the belt loops of his jeans and rather selfconsciously struck a pose. Sheila hid a smile at the belated show of masculine arrogance.

'Tell me,' she said, moving very close to him so that he would be able to smell her perfume and, possibly, be able to see down the front of her blouse. 'Do I make you nervous?'

His eyes – rather nice, grey eyes – widened momentarily, then he shrugged.

'Nervous? Of course not.'

'Good,' Sheila said briskly, moving away. 'Because I would very much like you to come over to my house and do a small job for me – perhaps when you have your break tomorrow lunchtime? I'd pay you for your time, of course.'

This was clearly not what he had been expecting and his bravado slipped.

'I . . . I don't know. I'll have to ask the foreman—'

'Oh, don't do that. We don't want the whole world and his wife to know, do we? I live at Rose Cottage – that's the first house you come to on Holly Lane. Do you know it?'

'Yes.'

'Yes, you know where it is, or yes, you'll come?'

He smiled, flashing even, white teeth at her.

'Both. I could be there for one, if that suits you?'

'One would be fine.' Smiling at him, Sheila turned away, then stopped in her tracks. 'Oh, I almost forgot! I'm Sheila.'

'Luke.'

'Until tomorrow then – Luke.'

She could feel his eyes following her as she walked through the pub towards the door, but she didn't look back. She had baited her hook; now all she had to do was wait to land the fish.

Putting the finishing touches to supper at number two, Alice paused, straining her ears. She could have sworn she heard a sound in the back garden of the house next door, not number one, but number three, on the other side. Tracy had told her that the Connors, who owned the house, spent much of the year abroad, which was why the house was empty.

Alice shrugged. It was probably a cat or something, nothing to worry about. Des called her from the living room to see something that had come on television and she went to join him, soon forgetting that she had thought she had heard anything at all.

The house felt empty when Sheila arrived home. She went straight upstairs for a shower, not allowing herself to wonder where her husband might be. After all, he wasn't in the least bit concerned how she spent her days, so she didn't see why she should beat herself over the head trying to work out what he was up to when he was away from her.

When she came out of the shower, she found that Rob had in fact been home, though he had obviously stayed only a short while. There was a large white cardboard box on the bed, with a card. Recognising her husband's bold italics, Sheila stood naked in the middle of the bedroom and picked it up.

'*For dinner at the Khans*',' she read, '*wear the red dress over the contents of the box, and your high-heeled red shoes. I'll be back to pick you up at seven – don't be late.*'

Sheila felt her stomach turn somersaults as she put the note aside. It had been a long time since Rob had initiated a game like this and she didn't entirely trust his motives. Had he a new mistress he wanted to impress by demonstrating his control over his wife? No, a new mistress would hardly be having dinner at the Khans'. It was a business meeting disguised as a social event. All that was required of Sheila was that she should sit quietly, and look decorative.

Her hands were trembling as she reached out for the lid of the box and opened it. Inside, lying across the expensive tissue paper wrappings, was a brand new riding crop.

Sheila swallowed, aware that the mere sight of the thing had made her grow wet and warm. She was shaking as she took it out and lay it across the pillow, on her side of the bed. The tissue paper rustled softly as she opened it. Her eyes widened as she reached in and picked out the bodysuit inside.

It was made of cool, shiny, black PVC lined with silk. There was hardly anything of it, a mere scrap of material which Sheila knew must have cost Rob more than a complete set of regular silk undies would have cost. It took her some moments to work out how to wear it. There were two holes for her legs, mere bands of fabric around her groin since her crotch and her mons were left exposed. At the back, it was cut high, to her waist, leaving her buttocks bare.

Easing it up over her waist, Sheila pushed her hands into the long, skintight sleeves and fastened the garment round her neck. Her breasts were restricted inside a band of PVC which clung to every line of her torso, so that she might as well be naked.

Going over to the wardrobe, Sheila found that it was difficult to bend down to pick up her shoes and she was panting by the time she straightened. Wiggling a little, she rearranged herself in the tight bodysuit before pushing her feet into the red, high-heeled court shoes. Taking her red dress off its hanger, she decided to check her underwear in the mirror before putting it on.

Standing before of the full length mirror on the front of her wardrobe, Sheila sucked in her breath. The outfit was incredible, moulding itself to every part of her that it covered. She could see the outline of her breasts, squashed against her ribcage in a bondage that bordered on the uncomfortable.

Framed by the black PVC thongs, her dark-haired mons looked shockingly exposed, the pink slit of her vulva just visible between her closed legs. Turning slowly, she saw that the fleshy, rounded globes of her buttocks were displayed to full advantage, their whiteness a stark contrast to the shiny black of the PVC and the caramel tan of the rest of her.

At least her husband still admired her figure, she thought to herself as she twisted this way and that. At forty-three Sheila had to work hard to keep her weight down to the level where she felt at her best, and for the past ten years she had worked out religiously, three times a week, at a small private gym in the city.

Her commitment had paid off for she had the figure of a

woman fifteen years younger. She supposed it had helped not having had children, but even so she was proud of the fact that it was mostly her own hard work that had kept her in trim, able to wear the kind of highly erotic outfit that she was studying now.

Bending slightly from the waist, Sheila imagined the white skin of her bottom striped with pink and almost came there and then. What was Rob playing at? Straightening, she pulled the red dress over her head. It was easy to see why Rob had chosen it – the long sleeves and high neckline concealed the bodysuit perfectly. It was a plain dress in bright red jersey which skimmed her body, right down to the floor. Its main feature was the back view – from the nape of her neck to the top of the split, which ended at mid-thigh, there were dozens of tiny buttons.

Now she knew exactly what Rob had in mind and she smiled to herself. She'd go along with it, this time. Her eyes fell on the riding crop lying across her pillow and she shivered. It was an image she knew would stay with her throughout the evening.

Rob walked through the door at seven o'clock precisely, to find Sheila waiting for him on the cream leather sofa. He watched as she stood up, noticing that, though she performed the manoeuvre with her usual grace, she winced slightly. So she had decided to wear his gift.

'I like your hair,' he said, his eyes caressing the lustrous dark hair piled up on Sheila's head.

'I put it up,' she said unnecessarily. 'I didn't want it to get in the way.'

Rob frowned at her. Sheila had never managed to grasp

the fact that talking about what was to take place took away much of the anticipation.

'Get your coat,' he said curtly. 'I'll wait for you in the car.' Ignoring her resentful glance, he strode out of the room.

Sheila fumed silently on the way to dinner. Who the hell did Rob think he was, talking to her like that? She glanced at him sideways. In profile, his face was sharp, almost hawk-ish, especially with his jaw clenched as it was now. Sheila could feel the barely suppressed anger in him and wondered at its cause. Rob had been restless lately, and easily pro-voked. She had given up trying to guess at what went on in his mind.

By the time they reached the house which belonged to his business client, he seemed to have softened slightly.

'I should have told you how lovely you look in that dress,' he said unexpectedly as he opened the car door for her and put out his hand.

Sheila looked from his hand to his face. Half of her wanted to prolong the frostiness between them, to punish him for his cavalier treatment of her. The other half was looking forward to the later part of the evening and did not want to risk Rob changing his mind. Putting her hand in his, she stepped out of the car.

'Thank you,' she replied quietly.

Rob smiled at her and she caught a glimpse of the young man with whom she had fallen in love not so very many years ago. Lifting her hand to his lips, he pressed a small, dry kiss at the join of her hand and thumb.

'Shall we?'

Sheila inclined her head and they walked up the steps to

the Khans' front door together.

The evening was long and uneventful, though Sheila was conscious of Rob's eyes on her as she moved about the room. The constriction across her breasts was quite uncomfortable now, and she was hot in the long-sleeved PVC. At dinner she was seated between an elderly relative of the client and a Frenchman whose English was fractured to say the least. Bored, Sheila longed to go home.

Later, as they had drinks in the high ceilinged drawing room, she tried to signal with her eyes across the room to Rob her eagerness to leave. He merely smiled at her and raised his glass. He must know she was uncomfortable, Sheila thought irritably. Even as she thought it she realised that this was part of his plan, that he derived pleasure from the idea that she was desperate to take the bodysuit off and be free of its constriction.

At last, the party was over. They drove home in silence, as they had arrived, but this time Rob seemed more relaxed.

'Did it go well?' Sheila ventured to ask as they pulled up outside their house.

'Well enough.'

Killing the engine, Rob turned to her in the darkness and smiled. Sheila sucked in her breath. She knew that smile. It was wolfish and calculated to make her pulse race. Without saying another word, she slipped out of the car and followed Rob to their front door. They went straight upstairs. Sheila reached out to turn on the light, but Rob put his hand over hers, stopping her.

'The moonlight will be sufficient,' he said, his lips close enough to her ear for her to be able to feel his warm breath across it.

The curtains were open and a shaft of silvery light fell across the bed. Moving so that she was standing in the light, Sheila was aware of the ghostly cast it lent her skin and she shivered as she imagined what Rob had in mind for her.

He was still standing in the shadows. Sheila could not see his expression, but she saw his tension in the way he held himself, taut. Something had clearly broken through his habitual ennui, for he wasn't behaving like the jaded man she knew him to be. Her eyes flickered from him to the riding crop and she felt a fluttering start up in her stomach.

'Turn around,' he said, his voice low.

Sheila did as he asked, slowly. All evening she had been kept on the verge of arousal, forced to behave normally while, underneath the respectable dress, she had been wearing a garment made purely for sex. Her breath seemed to hurt in her chest as she waited for Rob to make the next move.

'Aah!' she sighed as she felt his lips brush the delicate spot at the base of her skull. His fingers were gentle as he stroked the exposed curve of her neck and Sheila moaned softly.

'I love this dress,' he said, his voice throaty in her ear. 'I love the way it looks so demure one minute, and so tarty the next.'

He ran his hands down her arms, feeling the jersey slip against the PVC underneath. Sheila moaned and leaned back against him as he caressed the constricting band across her chest, lingering at her nipples which sprang to hardness under his fingers.

'Did you like my present?' he asked her.

'Mmm. It's tight, though.'

Rob chuckled against her hair.

'It's supposed to be tight. So that you can't forget you're wearing it.'

'Oh, I couldn't do that,' she admitted, revelling in the rhythmic slip of his palms over her breasts and across her stomach.

'How does it make you feel?'

'Hot.'

'Apart from hot.'

Sheila considered her answer for a moment.

'It makes me feel sexy . . . as if I'm just waiting . . .'

'For what?' he prompted when her voice faded away midsentence.

'For you.'

Rob kissed the side of her neck, his hands reaching down to polish the smooth mound of her pubis through the thin fabric of her dress.

'And what is it you are waiting for me to do?'

Sheila was breathing heavily now. Her mouth had run dry and she had to swallow hard before she could reply.

'I've been waiting for you to make me come.'

She felt Rob's lips curve against the dip of her shoulder.

'Of course. But now, my love? How do you want me to make you come?'

Sheila was torn between hating him for making her say the words aloud, and excitement because she knew that this was part of the game. It wasn't enough for her to submit physically, she had to surrender all of herself.

'With the crop,' she whispered.

Rob's fingers were kneading the pliant flesh of her belly, just above her bladder. Sheila felt a sudden need to pee and she held her breath, willing him to move downward, towards the cleft of her vulva.

'What was that, my love?' he whispered, his fingers toying with the sensitive area over her bladder. 'I didn't quite hear you.'

A whimper escaped through Sheila's lips and she leaned against him more heavily.

'I want you to whip me . . . please?'

Rob chuckled softly.

'Since you ask so nicely,' he mocked her.

His hands moved round her body to grasp the flesh of her bottom. Sheila felt a softening of the tender place between her legs as he squeezed the two halves of her buttocks, opening and closing them. She felt his fingers begin to unfasten the buttons of her dress from the waist down. When the dress was loose around her hips and legs, he stepped back from her.

'I want you on all fours,' he told her, 'on your hands and knees . . .'

Sheila complied with his wishes, though she felt foolish positioning herself on the floor like an animal. The soft fabric of her dress fell to either side of her waist, exposing the generous curves of her buttocks.

'You should see yourself, my love,' Rob said, his voice dreamy as he went over to the bed and picked up the riding crop. 'Such a perfect white arse, so soft and tempting . . . crawl over to the mirror so that you can see it.'

Sheila moved slowly on her hands and knees across the bedroom carpet. Once she was in front of the mirror, she looked back over her shoulder so that she could see the sight presenting itself to Rob. He was right – her bottom was a perfect white globe, pale in the moonlight. Rob reached down and stroked the softness of her skin and she sighed.

'How beautiful it will look, striped pink. Your skin is so cool to the touch – the crop will warm it.'

'Yes,' Sheila heard herself whisper.

'Good. Lift your bottom up higher please. Now, spread your knees apart so that I can see your sex. That's it. Beautiful. Even the thought of the crop has made you red and juicy.'

Sheila winced at his words even as they caused a fresh rush of moisture to overflow. The tension was unbearable and she willed him to get on with it. She heard the slap of the crop as Rob tested it against his own thigh and she almost came, there and then. Only the thought of Rob's disdain at her lack of control stopped her. Instead, she clenched her stomach muscles tightly and held her breath.

Everything seemed to happen in slow motion. From the corner of her eye, she saw Rob raise his arm. She heard the whistle as the crop sliced through the air, and the *thwack* as it made contact with her skin. She felt the searing heat across her buttocks, quickly tempering to a warm glow that seemed to travel right through her.

A second stroke took her by surprise and Sheila gave a long shuddering sigh. Resting her head on her folded arms, she raised her bottom higher to meet the sweet onslaught, allowing the wonderful release of submission to trickle through her as her buttocks were turned into a source of such heat she knew they must by now be flaming bright red.

Rob dropped the crop on the carpet beside her and placed a cool hand against her burning skin. Sheila groaned aloud, both at the pain occasioned by his touch and by the pleasure which followed swiftly in its wake.

'Up on the bed,' he told her, his voice hoarse.

Sheila moved quickly up on the bed, assuming the same position with her head resting on the pillows.

'Please?' she said when he didn't immediately join her. 'Rob?'

Twisting to look over her shoulder, she saw that he was still fully dressed. There was a look in his eye that she didn't quite trust and she frowned at him.

'Turn around,' he said harshly, 'and spread your legs wider.' He waited while she complied, then he slapped her, hard, across her glowing buttocks.

To her shame, Sheila immediately climaxed, her hips thrusting backwards as an explosion of sensation wracked her. Rob did not touch her again, he simply stood at the end of the bed and watched as she writhed in ecstasy.

After a few moments, she heard him walk over to the door.

'Rob?'

He paused.

'Stay in that position,' he instructed. 'Wait for me like that. Don't move an inch.'

Sheila heard the bedroom door close behind him and she buried her face in the pillows. They had played this game before. The waiting served only to heighten her sense of anticipation and after just a few minutes, she felt herself grow moist again, her labia swelling in expectation.

Would he take her from behind, or would he want her to feel the coolness of the sheets against her sore buttocks as he fucked her? Sheila closed her eyes as she imagined the satisfaction of having his thick strong cock filling her, taking her with him to new heights of pleasure.

It was some time before she realised that he wasn't coming back. Her arms and legs were aching, her sex had begun to dry and her back felt as though it might break. Face flaming with humiliation, Sheila climbed off the bed and undressed. Pulling her nightdress over her head, she covered it with her robe before going downstairs to confront Rob.

She found him in the living room, sitting in the dark with a glass of whisky at his elbow. Sheila stood in the open doorway and leaned against the frame.

'How long were you going to leave me there like that?' Her voice sounded flat and dull, unrecognisable even to her.

Rob looked towards her, but she gained the distinct impression that he wasn't really looking at her at all, but at some inner landscape to which she had no access.

'Well?' she prompted. 'Why didn't you come back?'

Rob focused on her for the first time and, to her fury, he smiled at her.

'I simply couldn't be bothered,' he drawled.

Sheila stared at him, torn between wanting to run away from him and wanting to fly at him and scratch at his handsome smug face.

'You bastard!' she whispered through lips that felt as though they were frozen into position.

Rob did not react; he merely picked up his glass and took a deep draught of whisky. Sheila watched him for a few moments more, then she turned and walked away.

Five

The day after the burglary, Andy came home unexpectedly, midmorning. He was carrying a large cardboard box from which he lifted a golden labrador pup. Tracy stared at it, attracted by its cute little face, but at a loss as to what to do with it.

'It's beautiful, Andy,' she said uncertainly, aware that he was disappointed with her lack of reaction. 'What's he called?'

'That's up to you,' he told her, 'it's your puppy. I thought he'd be company for you while I'm out at work all day, and when he's older and we've trained him, he'll be a good guard dog.'

Tracy smiled and went to kiss him. She was touched that Andy had thought of her and she decided there and then that she would overcome her fear of dogs to train the pup. After all, he was such a little thing – how could she be wary of him?

He wriggled as Tracy took him from Andy, but he didn't snap at her as she had feared he might, and he made no move to scramble out of her arms. She sat on the sofa with the dog on her lap and watched, fascinated, as he made himself comfortable and curled up.

The surge of protective feeling which she experienced when he laid his small head on his paws took Tracy by surprise. Andy watched her, unnerved by the uncharacteristic tenderness he felt towards her.

'So what are you going to call him?'

Tracy considered for a moment, caressing the dog's silky ears thoughtfully.

'Something short,' she said. 'Not fancy.'

'I've got to get back to work,' Andy told her, glancing at his watch. 'How about Rover?'

Tracy grinned at him.

'No way! You go to work and I'll let you know what I've decided tonight.'

Grinning, Andy bent his head to kiss her.

'You're beautiful when you smile like that,' he said, surprising himself. She did indeed look lovely, with her eyes shining, that awful anxious expression that was so often there banished for the moment. He felt a stab of guilt as he realised that it was he who had put that anxiety in her eyes. For the first time he wondered whether perhaps Tracy was no happier with their marriage than he. Immediately, he pushed the rogue thought away.

'There's a collar and lead in the box, and some puppy food,' he told her briskly. 'I'll see you later.'

Tracy got dressed in a pair of white jeans and a pale pink sweater. The puppy sat at her feet as she sat at her dressing table and watched as she applied her makeup. Unnerved by his unwavering scrutiny, she smiled at him.

'Are you hungry, dog?' she asked aloud.

The puppy put his head on one side and gazed at her with

its liquid brown eyes. Tracy thought it looked as though its mouth had lifted at the corners to return her smile.

'Maybe I should call you Smiler,' she said, leaning down to stroke the puppy's head. 'Or Sunny. Yes, I'll call you Sunny. You can cheer me up when I'm feeling miserable. Now, let's go and see if you're hungry, then we'll go out for our first walk together.'

It took Tracy a while to get used to walking Sunny on his lead – somehow he seemed to run around her feet and she became entangled several times. Turning right out of her driveway, she walked past Sheila's vast wooded garden before crossing by her gate. Turning right again, on to the main road, alongside the fence that bordered the Blakes' property, she reached the bridge across the river and paused, looking down at the murky water which passed underneath the road bridge.

To the right of the river as she looked at it was a footpath which led along the back of Rose Cottage, and her own house, number one, Holly Lane. Beyond that there were fields, through which the footpath followed the winding route of the river all the way to the next village, some two miles away.

Looking down at the restless little puppy dancing round her feet, Tracy decided that she would walk along the path as far as the fields, where he would be able to have a run.

The footpath was muddy and she picked her way along it in her unsuitable shoes, glad that Andy could not see her. Tracy was becoming increasingly fed up by Andy laughing at her, especially when, as now, she knew that she had made herself look foolish. Still, no one could see her now, mincing along a muddy footpath in white jeans and high-heeled shoes and she had to admit that she rather enjoyed the company of the little dog.

Passing the end of her own garden, she glanced over the fence, wondering if this could be how the burglar had managed to sneak into her home. She shivered, not wanting to think about it. In the distance, she saw a solitary figure walking on the footpath towards her, a man, though he wasn't close enough for her to see his face yet.

Her concentration interrupted for the moment, she was unprepared for Sunny's sudden tug on the lead, which slipped out of her hand as he went haring off towards the stranger.

'Sunny! Come back!'

The dog, not aware of his name yet, ignored her. Tracy saw the danger in the split second before the small puppy lost his footing and slipped down the steep riverbank and her shout carried along the towpath to the man approaching. He began to run, reaching the point where Sunny had disappeared at the same time as Tracy.

'Was it your dog? Where did he go?' he asked.

'Down there – oh, don't say he's been swept away!' Tracy was distraught, horror and guilt intermingling, rendering her helpless.

'No – look!' The man touched her arm and pointed to a mud bank on the river's edge, just below them.

Relief swamped her as Tracy saw that, rather than falling into the river, Sunny had landed on the mud bank. Being so small, though, he was unable to scrabble up the bank, and his increasingly frantic efforts made Tracy think that there was a very good chance that he could slither down into the cold water.

'Can you reach him?' she asked the man who had come to help her.

He turned to her and she saw he had the bluest, most thickly lashed eyes she had ever seen.

'Wait here,' he said.

Tracy watched as he jumped down on to the narrow mud bank and scooped the rapidly tiring puppy in his arms.

'Can you climb halfway down?' he called to her.

Tracy slid down the bank on the bottom of her white jeans and held out her arms for the pup. Sunny licked her face as she clasped him to her and she smiled, her eyes glittering with tears.

'Oh thank you, thank you!' she said to the man now climbing up the bank by her.

'Stay put, I'll give you a hand to get to the top.'

True to his word, he reached a hand down for her and hauled her, the dog still in her arms, up the bank. Scrabbling at the slippery soil, Tracy grabbed at the front of the stranger's donkey jacket to stop herself from sliding back down the bank. His arms came about her waist, steadying her, and she was conscious of their strength as they enclosed her. Looking up, their eyes met and for a moment time seemed to stand still.

Tracy held her breath, reading something in his eyes that she couldn't quite recognise. A kind of appreciation, a regard for her that she had seen once in Andy's eyes, but not, she realised now, for a long, long time. She blushed with confusion and saw him mask his expression quickly.

Sunny whimpered as he was crushed between them and broke the spell. They both looked down at the little dog and laughed at his plaintive expression.

'You'd best get him home and dry him off,' the man said, letting her go, 'he'll catch a chill.'

Tracy was disconcerted by how she missed the warmth of his arms around her and she covered her confusion by petting Sunny.

'I only live around the corner,' she told him, 'I'll go straight back. It was my fault – I'm not used to dogs. I don't know what my . . .' she trailed off, biting her lower lip. She was about to say she didn't know what her husband had been thinking of, buying her a dog when he knew she had no experience with them, but something stopped her. For some reason which she didn't care to analyse, she didn't want to tell the young man standing beside her that she was married.

He reached out now and stroked the puppy's head.

'You need to train him, for his own sake as well as yours.'

'I know. The trouble is, I don't know where to start. I suppose there must be a puppy training class somewhere nearby.'

'There is, over at Weston. I had a puppy when I was a boy and I took him there. I wouldn't be surprised if they're still there.'

'Oh. What happened to your puppy?'

'He lived to a ripe old age, then moved on to puppy heaven. Look, if you like, I could meet you here every afternoon and help you train this little rascal.'

'Don't you work?' Tracy asked him. He really did have the most beautiful eyes, she thought irrelevantly. She couldn't tell the colour of his hair since he was wearing a ski hat, pulled low over his ears. He was tall and fairly skinny, probably not much older than her, maybe a year or two.

'I've just dropped out of university. I'm going to take a year out before deciding what I want to do with my life.'

They began walking back towards the main road. Sunny squirmed in Tracy's arms, but she didn't dare put him down for fear of losing him again, this time possibly under the wheels of a car.

'That's very brave of you,' Tracy said.

'Giving up my degree?'

'Yes. It must have taken a lot of courage to decide you'd made a wrong choice.'

The man grimaced.

'I hope my parents will see it like that, though I doubt it, somehow! I'm Scott, by the way.'

'Tracy.' She smiled at him shyly. 'Did you mean it, what you said about helping me to train Sunny?'

'Absolutely. I could meet you at, say, two o'clock tomorrow afternoon, on the bridge?'

Tracy didn't hesitate for more than a second.

'All right. I'm turning left here,' she said as they reached the main road.

'I have to walk into town. See you tomorrow?'

'Yes. 'Bye.'

'Be seeing you. And you,' he added, tickling the top of Sunny's head.

Tracy watched him walk away. He had an easy, loose limbed gait, as if he hadn't a care in the world.

'Scott!' she called after him.

He paused and turned towards her.

'Thanks – for rescuing Sunny.'

He grinned at her.

'No problem. Cheerio.'

'Goodbye.'

She turned away and walked back towards Holly Lane feeling more lighthearted than she could remember feeling for a long, long time.

Sheila was wearing a simple shift dress in emerald green and medium-heeled courts dyed to match. At twelve forty-five she poured herself a glass of chilled white wine and moved to a seat where she could see out of the living room window, along the driveway of Rose Cottage.

She felt edgy and uncertain. Rob's behaviour last night had dented her sexual confidence and she was no longer so sure that Luke, the young builder working at the Dog and Duck, would come as arranged.

At one o'clock on the dot, she saw him walking up the driveway and breathed a sigh of relief. Moving away from the window so that he wouldn't catch sight of her and know that she had been waiting, she feasted her eyes on him. He was wearing a blue checked shirt and the same grubby jeans that he had worn the day before. His long, dirty-blond coloured hair was loose and looked soft and shiny, as if it had been freshly washed that morning. Sheila liked the way it rippled, imagining the feel of it under her fingers.

He paused as he reached the front door and Sheila saw that he looked nervous. Afraid that he might turn tail and run, Sheila hurried to the front door and opened it before he knocked.

'Luke – you're very punctual! I like that in a man. Come in.'

'I— you wanted me to look at some work that you need doing?'

Sheila cursed under her breath. In all the upset last night she had forgotten that she had invited him to the house on a ruse.

'Of course,' she said now. 'Come through – it's in the living room.'

Luke hesitated as he stepped through the door, glancing down at his thick working boots uncertainly.

'Perhaps you'd better take those off,' Sheila suggested, watching him as he untied the laces. She liked the idea of him leaving his boots by the door – in his socks he would feel more inclined to stay.

'Through here. I was thinking of having the stonework fireplace extended,' she improvised casually. 'Do you have any suggestions?'

Luke regarded Sheila's immaculate fireplace and raised his eyebrows.

'I . . . uh . . . I think it looks fine like that,' he mumbled after a moment.

'Do you?' Sheila moved so that she was standing very close to him. 'I thought, perhaps, you could make it longer, stretch it across to this wall . . .?'

Luke shook his head.

'It'd ruin the look of the room. No, I couldn't do it. It wouldn't be right.'

'Oh. Well, darling, I'm sorry to have wasted your time. Let me get you a drink to make up for it.'

'I'd better get back—'

'I insist.'

Luke looked down to where Sheila had placed her hand on his forearm and hesitated.

'Okay. I'll have whatever you're having.'

'White wine. I've got cold beer in the kitchen if you would prefer it?' she told him.

'Wine's OK, thanks.'

'Have a seat while I get you a glass.'

'I'd better stand – my jeans are filthy.'

There's a solution to that, Sheila wanted to say. *You won't be in them for long – why not take them off now?* Aloud she said, 'Don't worry about that. I'll be two minutes. Don't go away!'

When she returned with a fresh glass of wine, Luke seemed much more relaxed than he had when he first arrived. As he took the glass from her, their fingers touched and he caught her eye. Sheila was relieved to see desire written in them, but there was something else, an uncertainty that excited her far more than the confirmation that he found her attractive. Instinct told her that this young man was far less experienced than he liked to make out and her interest in him sharpened.

'You've got a nice house, Sheila,' he said, raising his glass to her before drinking from it.

'Thank you. Perhaps you'd like to have a look round?' It would be one way of getting him upstairs without wasting too much time.

Luke followed her up the stairs. Sheila could feel his eyes on her bottom and she wondered what his reaction would be when he saw the pale pink stripes patterning the smooth white skin. She shivered.

Making a show of taking him from room to room, she was gratified to sense the tension building in him as they came to the master bedroom. He knew what he was here for, but he was clearly leaving it to her to set the pace.

'And this is where I sleep,' she said as they walked into the cool blue and grey bedroom, 'or otherwise . . .'

Luke's eyes flickered from her face to the big double bed and back again. He was standing very close to her and his eyes glittered as he regarded her.

'Are you sure about this?' he asked, watching her carefully.

'Of course.'

He stared at her for a moment longer, then he leaned forward and kissed her.

It was a hot kiss, open mouthed and unembarrassed. Sheila coiled her arms around his neck and pulled him closer, moulding the softness of her body against the hard planes of his. She could feel his erection, hot and vibrant, pressing against the constriction of his jeans and she knew that he was as excited as she.

'Why don't you get undressed?' she murmured thickly.

Luke did not need to be asked twice. Sheila backed towards the bed, her eyes never leaving him as he pulled off his shirt and his jeans. His body was well-built and bronzed from working outside all summer long. Sheila watched the play of muscles beneath the vibrant, youthful skin as he bent down to disentangle himself from his jeans and felt a pulse of pure pleasure begin to beat between her thighs.

He moved towards her, unselfconsciously naked, his smooth, straight cock pointing straight at her. Sheila revelled in the unrestrained passion she could see in his eyes as he stopped inches away from her. She loved this moment, when a young man could still hold himself back, teetering on the brink of losing control.

She could sense his tension, see that every muscle was

taut, barely kept in check. Smiling slowly, she curled her fingers under the hem of her shift, pulling it over her head and flinging it aside.

She was naked underneath it. Surprise flared in Luke's eyes, swiftly chased away by desire. Sheila stood proudly in front of him, knowing that, despite the difference in their years, there was nothing about her body that could possibly displease him.

'Shit, you're gorgeous,' he breathed.

It was hardly the most romantic of compliments, but Sheila took it in the spirit in which it was intended and reached out for him. They kissed, deeply, and she felt for the first time the thrill of his naked skin against hers. He was warm and his skin felt like damp velvet as it slipped against hers.

His hands roved her body quickly, caressing her breasts and her waist before the fingers of one hand curled into the hot, damp cleft of her vulva. Sheila felt his fingers sink into her wetness and closed her eyes. Her entire body seemed to tremble as he explored the hot, wet folds of her sex, his touch almost clumsy in his urgency. He found her clitoris which seemed to buzz with feeling as he ground it against his fingerpad.

Luke's cock twitched against Sheila's stomach and she felt a warm, sticky fluid smear her skin. He kissed her fervently, making up in enthusiasm what he lacked in finesse, all the while rubbing at her clitoris with an enthusiasm that bordered on the painful.

Suddenly, he seemed to lose control completely. Pushing her back on the bed, he pushed her thighs apart and nudged at the entrance to her body with the tip of his cock.

'Wait!' Sheila said, taken by surprise.

Reaching into the drawer of her bedside table, she took out one of the condoms she had unwrapped earlier and rolled it quickly over his penis, before he had time to object. In fact, Luke was beyond objecting to anything. As soon as she removed her fingers, he thrust into her, covering her body with his so that she sank into the softness of the mattress. With a muttered exclamation, he fucked her energetically.

Carried away by his uninhibited enthusiasm, Sheila quickly reached a climax. Despite his inexpert handling of her clitoris, she was suffused with warmth, every nerve ending zinging, quivering with pleasure. Her internal muscles spasmed around his marauding cock, precipitating his own orgasm.

'Jesus! Oh shit!' he gasped as he collapsed across her, his mouth seeking hers in a blind expression of emotion.

Sheila waited until he had rolled off her before reaching for the Kleenex she kept on the side and handing him one. She also lit up two cigarettes and handed him one of those. After recovering for a few minutes, Luke propped himself up on one elbow and watched her as they smoked. He looked so pleased with himself, endearingly smug, in fact, and Sheila felt quite tender towards him.

When she had finished her cigarette, she stubbed it out in the ashtray by the bed and smiled at him.

'Are you OK?' she asked him solicitously.

'Yeah. Are you?' Some of the confidence slipped from his eyes. 'I mean . . . it was all right, wasn't it? For you, I mean . . .?'

Smiling, Sheila reached forward to smooth a lock of hair

which had fallen across his eye from behind his ear.

'It was lovely,' she said kindly. 'For starters.'

Indignation passed across his features, mingled with uncertainty.

'You don't have to rush off, do you?' she asked him, making her voice low and seductive. 'I mean, it would be a shame to waste the mood we've created, wouldn't it? A young man like you wouldn't be satisfied with a quick shag, would you?'

Luke nodded, decidedly uncomfortable now.

'Well, I—'

'I know what it's like, darling, believe me. I know a great deal about young men like you. Most of the time you have to rush, get the job done before the girlfriend's parents come down the stairs and catch you at it; snatch a quick knee trembler in a back alley . . . that's why it would be so nice if you stayed . . .'

Sheila allowed her fingers to walk down his body to his lap. His limp cock stirred as she brushed against it and she smiled, stroking it lovingly as it gradually grew hard again.

'There,' she said softly, 'almost ready to start again.'

Glancing at him she saw his pupils dilate and knew she hadn't misread him.

'Have you ever been with an older woman before, Luke?'

He shook his head and his adam's apple bobbed as he swallowed hard.

'I thought not. You see, with an older woman you don't have to rush, in fact, the longer you spend before and after, the better we like it. Younger women aren't that different, for that matter, darling. We all like to spend time on our pleasures. Let me show you . . .'

Leaning forward, she pressed her lips against his. Luke lay back on the pillows and closed his eyes as she insinuated her tongue between his teeth and began to explore the inside of his mouth. Now that the initial urgency had receded, Sheila knew he would be able to appreciate more leisurely delights. He tasted of cherries and tobacco and Sheila took her time, kissing him deeply, then running her tongue lightly around the sensitive inner surface of his lips.

Sheila could feel a smooth, liquid warmth seeping through her limbs as she sat up and looked down at him. Her eyelids drooped as she ran her fingertips across the velvet softness of his skin, tracing the outline of his collarbone and sweeping down to circle his pectorals. Tracing ever decreasing circles on the surface of his skin, she played with the soft brown disc of his nipple until the flesh puckered, the tip inviting her kiss.

Luke shuddered as Sheila pressed the flat of her tongue against the small promontory, making her smile.

'You see?' she whispered huskily, her tongue tracing the whorls of his ear. 'There's more to erogenous zones than six inches between your thighs.' She bit gently on the fleshy lobe of his ear and his breath escaped through his lips on a sigh.

Sheila sat up and gazed down at him, feasting her eyes on the youthful glow of his skin, admiring the sculpted symmetry of his body. Like a child in a sweet shop, she felt overwhelmed, not knowing where to start. Luke lay passively watching her, a slight wariness in his eyes.

'You . . . you're not going to do any kinky stuff, are you?' he asked her.

Sheila laughed aloud.

'*Kinky stuff?* Darling, how prissy you are these days! What is it you're afraid of?' she asked him, leaning forward confidingly. 'Is it pain?' She laughed at the alarm that crossed his face. 'Don't worry,' she said, taking pity on him. 'We're not going to do anything in this room that makes you feel uncomfortable. All right?'

Luke nodded, the faintest of smiles touching his lips.

'That's better. Now – how would you feel about giving me a rather special massage?'

She climbed off the bed and backed away from him, taking care that he didn't see the marks of the crop on her buttocks. She didn't want to scare him off completely. In the top drawer of her chest of drawers, she kept a small bottle of almond-scented massage oil.

Luke took it from her, obviously intrigued.

'You rub it in, darling – all over my breasts and between my legs. On you too, if you like. It'll give you a sensation quite unlike anything you'll ever have experienced before, believe me.'

Lying on her back on the pillows, she gathered up the soft mounds of her breasts in her hands and pointed them at him.

'Do you like my breasts?' she asked him conversationally.

Luke flushed a little, though he couldn't seem to take his eyes off the rapidly hardening areolae.

'They . . . they're very nice,' he agreed, fumbling with the screw top of the massage oil.

'That's it, darling – slosh it on. The more you use, the better the effect.'

Sheila raised her arms above her head and stretched like a cat as Luke laid his oily hands on her breasts. Clumsily at first, he began to work the fragrant oil into her skin, concentrating on the puckered skin of her areolae.

'Slowly,' she instructed him softly, 'long strokes . . . mmm!'

Luke was a quick learner and before too long Sheila had him oiling her upper body like an expert masseur. The expensive special ingredient in the massage oil made her skin tingle all over, her nipples prickling, two supersensitive bundles of nerve endings sending signals direct to her clitoris.

Sheila was aware that Luke would never have had the patience to service her like this had she asked him before he had come the first time, but now his rearousal was slow enough to allow him to enjoy the foreplay almost as much as she. Even so, by the time his fingers slipped lower, his erection was straining towards her, his cock like a totem, pointing straight up to his heart.

He was breathing heavily, his eyes wide with curiosity as he watched Sheila's reaction to the massage. As his fingers touched the fringe of her pubic hair, Sheila allowed her heels to slip apart on the cool cotton sheet, exposing her most private of places to his eager young eyes.

As he pushed her thighs wider apart and peered at her, Sheila liked to think that she was teaching him something that he would be able to carry into his future relationships, something about giving that would benefit his future girlfriends. But that was in the future – right now all that Sheila wanted was for his fingers to follow the path of his gaze preferably smeared with the magical elixir in the small, unmarked bottle.

She shuddered as he spilt the oil along the cleft of her

vulva, working it into the already slippery channels on either side of her labia with a thoroughness which she applauded.

'Oh, you're good darling!' she moaned. 'Now rub my clit for me . . . yes! Turn around – I want your cock in my mouth.'

Luke moved so fast that no sooner had she finished speaking than she found herself at eye level with the straight, strong shaft of his penis. Little shards of delight were radiating out from her clitoris as he stroked it in a slow, circular motion that was destined to drive her wild.

Putting out her tongue, Sheila traced the underside of his prick, caressing his balls with her fingertips until she found the potent, secret spot behind them that would hasten his climax, when required. First, though, she wanted to taste him and she stretched her lips wide over the bulbous tip of his penis, drawing the length of him into her mouth and sucking gently.

'Shit!' Luke breathed, trembling with the effort of holding himself back as Sheila began to fellate him like a connoisseur. Her sex, open and liquid, was mere inches from his face, her clitoris literally pulsing before his eyes. Tentatively, he pressed his tongue against it, and immediately tasted the almond flavour of the oil she had given him to massage into her. It made his tongue tingle and he swirled his tongue all around her sex, lapping at the places where he had smeared the oil.

Sheila realised that he was doing his utmost not to come in her mouth. She was close to climax herself and she was determined that they should reach the peak more or less simultaneously. She was also determined that she should be able to swallow the reservoir of semen she envisioned building at the base of his cock and she sucked harder, drawing it to the point of no return.

Her own climax started slowly, with a quivering in her clitoris that gradually grew into a vibration that travelled throughout her body. As soon as she felt the deeper tremors building in her vagina, she pressed firmly at the small, sensitive pad of flesh behind Luke's scrotum, whilst at the same time she sucked rhythmically at the shaft.

'Uh . . . uh . . . I can't stop . . .' Luke gasped as the first hot jag of seed pumped out of his body and into Sheila's waiting mouth.

He pressed his lips against her throbbing clitoris and drew it into his mouth, mimicking the way she was sucking him until he felt her quiver anew and a fresh orgasm surged through her, taking her by surprise. By the time they broke apart, they were both panting, covered in perspiration. Their eyes met and they grinned.

'A shower, I think, when we've caught our breath?' Sheila suggested.

Luke nodded, too overcome for the moment to respond.

In the shower, Sheila soaped him gently all over, paying special attention to the now flaccid tube of his cock. Luke returned the compliment, washing away every last trace of the oil from her breasts and fingering the sore, tender folds of flesh between her legs with gentle fingers. Already he was far more confident about the way he touched her, was far more considerate of how each caress would feel and Sheila was proud of his progress. Hopefully, he would be willing to come back, for a little while, so that he could graduate from the Sheila Blake school of the sexual arts!

Luke paused as he saw the faded stripes on her buttocks and he looked as though he might ask her how she had come by them. Without a word, Sheila put her fingers to his lips and shook her head. She didn't want to discuss her relationship with her husband with him, and though she could sense his curiosity, it was really none of his business.

The water ran over them and between them in a continuous warm stream, plastering Luke's long hair to his forehead, making him look very young. Sheila felt herself stirring yet again.

Moving closer to him, she felt the slight hardening of his penis and knew that he too would be ready again, very soon. Trapping him against the wall with her upper body, she began to kiss him, revelling in the feeling of his cock growing against her belly.

She gasped as, suddenly, he grasped the initiative and lifted her off her feet. Turning her, he reversed their positions so that now she was leaning with her back against the cool, wet tiles and his thigh was between her legs, rubbing against the hot crevice of her vulva.

His eyes were hot on her as he gazed down at her, his expression fixed as he battled to restrain himself. Sheila saw the turmoil in the back of his eyes and smiled. She wanted him to use that primitive urge, to take her, savagely, the way he so clearly wanted.

'Yes,' she breathed, 'do it Luke – do it now!'

It was all the encouragement he needed. Putting his hands on her waist, he lifted her and, using the tiled wall as a support, he lowered her on to the upright staff of his cock.

Sheila cried out, burying her face in his shoulder as his cock speared her. Her arms came around his shoulders, her legs folded around his waist and she rocked her pelvis back and forth, deepening his penetration.

'Harder!' she cried.

Luke grunted as he pushed her against the wall and thrust into her as hard and as deeply as he could. Their eyes locked in silent battle, each determined to last the distance, neither satisfied with gentleness any more.

They slid together down the wall until Sheila was lying on the floor of the shower, warm water flowing over her face, in her mouth and ears and eyes, unheeded as Luke slammed into her, over and over, until she was sore.

His face contorted in a rictus of ecstasy as, at last, his climax overtook him and he pulled out of her just in time, jetting his seed on to the shower floor, to be swirled down the plughole with the water.

'Good boy,' Sheila said approvingly when she had regained sufficient energy to speak.

Without a word, Luke stood up and turned off the shower. He held out his hand to Sheila and helped her to dry herself on a big fluffy towel, fresh from the airing cupboard. They walked together into the bedroom where Luke dressed, still in silence. It was Luke who finally broke it.

'Can I see you again?'

Sheila went over and kissed him on the cheek.

'I'll count on it. After all, that was only the beginning, darling, wasn't it?'

She chuckled softly as Luke blanched, stroking the side of his face with her palm.

'You'd best get back to work, or I'll be losing you your job. Leave your phone number on the pad by the telephone in the hall – I'll ring you next week.'

He nodded and, with one last kiss, he left her alone in the bedroom. Moving over to the window, Sheila watched as he walked along the driveway. Some of the spring had gone from his step, but he looked happy, as if he owned the world. That's how she liked her men to leave her bedroom – feeling they could conquer nations!

Smiling, Sheila lay back on the bed. The sheets smelled of Luke and of sex. Wrapping herself in them, she closed her eyes and quickly fell into a deep, dreamless sleep.

Six

'I don't know how you can have failed to notice my clock was missing,' Sonja said, pouting at Liz as she undressed ready for bed.

Liz flushed.

'I had more important things on my mind,' she snapped.

'That clock was valuable – you should have told the police about it.'

'You can ring them yourself and have it put on the list together with my five hundred quid.'

Sonja tutted loudly, turning away to drop the clothes she had taken off in the washing basket.

'I don't know what you were thinking of, keeping that amount of money in the house.'

'I was saving it,' Liz replied, climbing into bed and pulling the covers up to her chin in a protective gesture that was not lost on Sonja. Hardening her heart, she chose to ignore it.

'Banks, not bedside tables, are for savings.'

'It was for your birthday.'

'What?' Sonja instantly felt guilty, which is probably what Liz had intended all along, she thought resentfully. She slipped between the covers on her side of the bed and regarded Liz in the semi-darkness. 'What on earth were you thinking of buying me with that kind of money?' she asked.

She hadn't meant her tone to be quite that cutting, but nevertheless she was irritated when she detected a swallowed sob in Liz's voice when she answered her.

'I saw a ring in the window of the jewellery shop in town. It was so beautiful . . . I knew you'd like it, and I wanted to get you something really special . . .'

Sonja sighed. She could feel Liz waiting for her to roll across the cold gap between them in the bed and make things right between them again, but she knew that it wasn't what she wanted, not any more.

'Liz . . . we've got to talk.'

'Must we?' Liz answered, her voice small.

'I think so. This is all so . . . so demeaning.'

'For you? Or for me?'

'For both of us,' Sonja said softly. 'Look, Liz, you know it's against everything you believe in to spend all that money on a piece of jewellery. Where did you get the money from anyway?'

Liz shifted uncomfortably in the bed.

'I've been doing some work on the allotment next to mine – ours. I—'

'No, Liz,' Sonja interrupted her, 'you were right the first time. It's *your* allotment, not ours. Your house. Your dream.'

'I thought it was yours too.'

Sonja felt her heart squeeze in her chest as she detected the unhappiness in Liz's voice.

'No,' she replied, knowing that she was tolling a death

102

knell for their relationship with her honesty. 'It never was. I'm sorry.'

It was some moments before Liz spoke again, and when she did, Sonja could tell she was battling with herself to keep the tears in check.

'I see.'

Her voice was horribly small.

'I'm sorry, Liz,' Sonja repeated, feeling quite upset herself now that she had initiated the conversation.

'What are you going to do?'

Sonja sighed heavily.

'I think it would be best if I moved out – made a clean break, don't you?'

Liz felt the panic rear up to swamp her and she fought it back. Pride would not let her show Sonja how much she was hurting.

'Where will you go?'

Sonja's tone was guarded as she told her.

'Lulu and JD have said they can put me up, just temporarily, until I can find a place of my own. I don't want you to think . . . well, it is just temporary.'

Liz felt the waves of despair pounding at her and concentrated hard on breathing in through her nose, out through her mouth.

'I see,' she said at last. 'You don't have to move out immediately, though, Sonja – you can stay here until you find somewhere.' Liz despised herself for the note of desperation she detected in her own voice and she was unsurprised when Sonja stuck by her decision.

'I think it would be better if I went tomorrow.'

Better for whom? Liz thought silently. So much for a clean break – if Sonja was going to be living just next door, where Liz was bound to keep bumping into her and imagining . . . she simply couldn't see how she would be able to bear it.

They lay together in the darkness, each wakeful for her own differing reasons. Gradually, Sonja's hand found Liz's across the chasm between them and their fingers entwined.

'I don't want you to think I don't care,' she whispered. 'It's been fun. But it wasn't meant to be a forever thing, y'know?'

Liz squeezed her hand, not trusting herself to speak for a moment.

'Forever's a long time,' she replied at last.

'Yeah,' Sonja agreed. 'A hell of a long time.'

Disentangling her hand gently from Liz's, she rolled over and made herself comfortable, leaving Liz staring at the darkened ceiling, feeling more alone than she'd ever felt before in her entire life.

Des Grainger watched as Alice brushed her hair in front of the dressing table mirror. The light was behind her, illuminating the shape of her body beneath the demure white nightdress, catching her unawares.

Des had an erection, the frustrations of the day before stroking his lust to the point where he just didn't know how much longer he could wait. Somehow, Alice had managed to be asleep by the time he had showered and crawled into bed beside her the night before, and nothing he did seemed to wake her. He had been desperate, but not so desperate that he didn't want her to be awake while they made love!

It was all right for Alice – she had enjoyed what appeared to be one of the best orgasms of her life yesterday before

Tracy from next door had arrived and interrupted them. If he closed his eyes, he could picture her now, abandoned to him as he'd never seen her before. And all because of the champagne on an empty stomach – he'd have to remember it affected her like that!

Opening his eyes, Des watched Alice walk towards him and slip beneath the covers. He waited until she'd leaned over to switch off the light before reaching for her.

'Not now, Des,' she said, yawning. 'I'm whacked.'

'But Alice—'

'Just go to sleep, can't you? All you ever think about is sex. If you're that desperate, why don't you go and relieve yourself in the bathroom or something?'

Speechless with indignation, Des stared at the back Alice had presented to him in the darkness. His cock twitched, an uncomfortable reminder of the desert that was his sex life. All that there was left for him to do was to twist violently on to his side, away from her, leaving a cold tunnel of air between them under the duvet.

Meanwhile, next door at number one, Tracy was bound to the iron bedhead while Andy thrust in and out of her. It felt like he had been at it for hours; it had been a long time since she had come and now she just wanted him to get it over with.

Andy was perspiring heavily, his skin shiny in the dim lighting of the bedroom. Though he was looking straight at her, his eyes were unfocused and Tracy guessed he was locked into some secret fantasy world of his own, a world from which she was excluded. She thought of Scott, the man she had met on the river path. Somehow she doubted if he would make love to her like this. He would make love with all of himself, would give himself wholeheartedly to her . . . *what was she thinking of?*

Glancing guiltily at Andy, she saw that he was nearing his climax, at last. He was oblivious to where Tracy's thoughts might be, she was free to send them wherever she wanted.

She could hear Sunny whimpering in the utility room, where Andy had put the basket he had brought home for him. She had wanted to bring the puppy into their room, but Andy said he had to learn to be alone at night.

Andy came, grunting as he collapsed over her. After a few minutes, he untied her, automatically rubbing her wrists and pulling the duvet up over them.

'That was fantastic, baby,' he murmured as he slipped into sleep.

Tracy lay and listened to the sound of his breathing, becoming more regular, deeper. When she finally closed her own eyes it was Scott's face she saw imprinted on the insides of her eyelids. She'd be seeing him again tomorrow. Only a few short hours away. And she knew she couldn't wait.

At number five, JD stirred in his sleep and pulled Lulu closer to him. Her body, in the baby doll pyjamas she always wore, seemed to fit against him as if they were two parts carved from the same sculpture. JD smiled as the sleepy thought occurred to him. Lord, he was a lucky man!

Lulu wriggled against him and curled her fingers over his in her sleep. Contented and secure, JD quickly fell asleep again.

Downstairs, the intruder stood in the middle of the living room and listened. The house was sleeping, the time marked by the sonorous ticking of an old grandfather clock in the corner of the room.

This house was different from the others. Like an Aladdin's cave, it was stuffed full of antiques and curiosities which JD had collected during the years he had spent living in Africa and India. Many of the items were too easily traceable to steal, though they made the intruder's mouth water just to look at them. It took a while to select the best pieces to take. Now for the favourite part.

The stairs creaked slightly under the burglar's weight, provoking a pause. No one stirred. Inside the bedroom where JD and Lulu slept, the intruder located the chest of drawers in the darkness and tiptoed over.

Ah, this was a silk and lace woman, a woman whose underwear reflected her femininity. Whereas the contents of some women's lingerie drawers turned up surprises, it appeared that this woman wore exactly what one would expect her, given her outward appearance, to wear under her clothes.

The intruder selected a bra and briefs' set by touch alone and pushed it into the bag slung over one shoulder.

'What the blazes is going on!'

The intruder whirled round to see the Colonel sitting bolt upright in bed. Heart hammering, the burglar turned tail and ran. JD sprang out of the bed and fumbled for his old army revolver which he kept ready and loaded in his bedside drawer for just such an occasion. Pounding, barefoot, down the stairs, he ran out of the open front door, ignoring Lulu's frantic shouts for him to come back.

Outrage lent wings to his feet as he pursued the thief along the driveway and out onto the road.

'Stop where you are, or I'll shoot!' JD yelled at the figure, now no more than a shadow, running through the pub car park which was beside the house, heading for the main road.

Adopting a combat stance, he took aim just above the figure's head and fired three times.

'JD! JD – stop it! Please!'

JD looked round, feeling dazed, as he heard Lulu sobbing behind him.

'Damn reprobate got clean away!' he said.

'Come inside, JD – leave it to the police. Please, darling – come inside.'

JD allowed Lulu to steer him back into the house. He gradually became aware that the lights had gone on in the house next door and in numbers one and two opposite. They all must have seen him fail to protect his home and his wife. They'd all see him exactly for what he was, an impotent, useless old man with an outdated revolver, standing in the middle of the street in the dark, wearing his pyjamas. It was some minutes before he realised that the wetness he could feel on his face was the result of tears.

'So then the police interviewed everyone who'd come out to see what was going on, and poor JD was given a dreadful ticking off about keeping a loaded revolver in the house.' Tracy glanced at Scott, catching his eye. He was laughing quietly at the scene she had just described and she joined him, hugging the pleasure of making him laugh to herself with silent glee.

'It's a good job the old boy didn't hit the intruder when he fired. He'd probably have found himself in the dock,' Scott commented grimly.

They were walking towards the next village having succeeded in teaching Sunny to trot along beside Tracy's feet. The sun was shining and Tracy, dressed in jeans and a pair of loafers, felt far more comfortable than she had the day before. Scott turned his head and smiled at her, and she experienced the same jolt of feeling she had felt when she saw him waiting for her on the bridge earlier.

'I'm glad you came,' he said now, lowering his eyelids to mask his sudden awkwardness. 'I wasn't sure that you would.'

Tracy gazed at him incredulously. This unexpected admission of insecurity endeared him to her far more than any false confidence would and, impulsively, she slipped her arm through his.

'I said I would, didn't I?' she said, not adding that she had had exactly the same fears about him.

They walked arm in arm through the small spinney that marked the halfway point on the footpath between the two villages. As they emerged through to the other side, Scott stopped walking and turned Tracy in his arms. She knew that he was about to kiss her, just as she knew that she should stop him, before it was too late. Somehow, she couldn't seem to move; she simply stood and waited for the first touch of his lips against hers.

They were warm and firm, tantalising her gently as he took her into his arms. Tracy closed her eyes and leaned in towards him, breathing in the woody, masculine scent of his skin as his mouth moved to the sensitive area behind her ear.

Sunny whimpered suddenly beside her and Tracy broke away.

'What's wrong?' Scott asked, not allowing her to pull away from him completely.

'I . . . I can't,' Tracy whispered, avoiding his eye.

'You can't what? You can't kiss me? You can't walk with me?'

'No. I can't do any of those things. I'm sorry, I should have told you right from the start. I'm married, Scott.'

'I know.'

Tracy's eyes flew up to meet his as his words took her by surprise.

'You know?' she repeated. 'But how . . .?'

Scott smiled at her and lifted her left hand to his lips. His mouth grazed the thin gold wedding band on her finger and Tracy blushed.

'Of course. How stupid of me.'

Scott frowned darkly.

'I don't think you're stupid, Tracy.'

'No?' She smiled bitterly. 'Everybody else does.'

'Everybody else being your husband, I presume?'

Tracy glanced at him in surprise.

'Well, yes.'

They began walking again, and Tracy gathered that Scott intended to stick to their original plan to carry on as far as the pub in the next village.

'You don't mind?' she ventured after a few minutes. Her hand was still held fast in Scott's, and she found herself enjoying its warmth.

'No, I don't mind. It would be different if you were happy.'

'What makes you think I'm not happy with Andy?' she asked, not sure she liked his easy self assurance that he knew her that well already.

'You wouldn't be here with me now if you were happily married,' he said simply. 'Would you?'

Tracy hesitated briefly before she replied.

'I suppose not,' she admitted after a moment.

'Well, then. Let's enjoy the rest of the afternoon shall we? Then tomorrow, if you still want to, we'll meet again and carry on with Sunny's training.'

Tracy smiled, leaning her head briefly against Scott's shoulder.

'I want to,' she said softly.

On Friday morning, Alice came out of the back of the small supermarket which was part of the parade of shops on the main road, next to the Dog and Duck. She intended to cut through the pub car park on to Holly Lane, but, glancing towards the allotments to her right, she recognised the woman who lived at number four, and decided to go and introduce herself.

'Hi,' she said over the fence. 'You're Liz, aren't you?'

Liz stopped what she was doing and nodded.

'I'm Alice Grainger – I've just moved in across the road from you.'

'Oh yes – pleased to meet you.'

Wiping her muddy hands on the back of her fatigue pants, Liz walked over to the fence.

'You have a good sized plot there – do you work it all by yourself?'

Liz gave a small, rueful smile. As she came closer, Alice

saw the lines of strain etched around her thoughtful grey eyes and wondered what had put them there.

'Yes,' she said. 'I grow all our – my – own vegetables. I took on the allotment as an extension to the garden, really.'

'Do you cultivate your garden too?' Alice asked, her interest quickening.

'Yes. It's an all-consuming interest of mine, the pursuit of self sufficiency.' She gave a small, self-deprecating laugh the reason for which Alice did not understand.

'The soil looks good anyway. Do you use fertilisers?'

'Only those I produce myself, all natural. Are you interested in gardening?' she asked curiously. 'Only, most people's eyes glaze over at the mere mention of my allotment, never mind asking questions.'

Alice grinned.

'I was brought up on a smallholding.'

Liz's face lit up.

'No kidding? Where?'

'On the border between England and Wales. My father is still there.'

Liz looked at Alice with dawning respect.

'How could you bear to leave it? That's my long-term aim – to move to a place with enough land to be really self sufficient.'

'I visit Dad as often as I can and, I have to admit, I do miss it. Maybe I could come and see your garden sometime?'

Liz shrugged.

'Are you free now?'

Alice's face split into a wide smile.

'I could be. Let me just take these groceries home and change into something more practical,' she suggested, glancing down at her sundress and sandals. 'I could be over in twenty minutes, if that's all right with you?'

'That'd be great. I'll put the kettle on.'

Liz regarded Alice speculatively as she walked across the car park. Hadn't there been a man with her when she moved in? Liz frowned. It didn't matter – even if Alice was only interested in friendship, it would be wonderful for Liz to be able to share her passion for the good life with someone of a like mind. Turning away, she gathered up her tools and picked up the wheelbarrow, whistling softly under her breath.

The Holly Lane burglar sat back in an armchair at home and replayed the events of the night before. JD McFarlane was as mad as a hatter! When he'd fired that pistol, he must have known he could have killed his target.

It had been a close shave. Not only had the physical danger become very real, but the police had taken a sudden interest in the goings on in the Lane. Three burglaries and an attempted assault by a householder – it was lucky the papers hadn't got hold of it, or the game would have been well and truly up.

Maybe it was time to stop. The intention was never to be hurt, or even to hurt the victims. But the new people at number two hadn't received a visit yet, and then there was the Connors' house at number three, standing empty, just waiting to be plundered. The alarm system there was a challenge to be relished.

No, it wasn't time to give up, not yet. There was too much fun still to be had.

Liz poured out two cups of apricot tea and handed one to Alice. They had spent a pleasant hour touring the garden and Alice had asked a multitude of intelligent questions that had allowed Liz to give full vent to her passion – for gardening, that is. Her rapidly growing interest in Alice herself was something that she studiously kept in check.

It was probably just a rebound thing, what with Sonja moving out only that morning and the way she had been feeling so low in herself lately. Sitting at the opposite end of the kitchen table to Alice, Liz studied her surreptitiously over her mug.

She wasn't exactly pretty, certainly not in Sonja's league, but there was an attractiveness about Alice's face which came from within. Her light skin glowed with the delicate tone of her freckles, which looked like pale paint spots randomly applied to her face. Her fair hair was slightly frizzy at the ends and she had the most exquisitely shaped eyebrows which framed her eyes to perfection.

Her eyes were probably her best feature. A clear, periwinkle blue, they were so expressive that Liz wondered fleetingly if Alice was aware of quite how revealing they were. They were animated now as she talked of her childhood on the smallholding and Liz's eyes lingered on her mouth, noticing that her lower lip was slightly fuller than the top one, giving the impression of a permanent pout.

Now she was saying how much she missed the simple tasks that had been hers when she lived with her father, and complimenting Liz on her efficiency.

'Well, you know you'd be welcome to come and give me a hand any time the mood takes you.'

'Really?' Alice looked genuinely delighted with Liz's half tongue-in-cheek offer. 'I know it sounds crazy, but sometimes I yearn for the sensation of soil under my fingernails!'

The two women smiled at each other, sharing a moment of perfect accord.

'Tell me,' Liz said, putting her mug down carefully in front of her on the table, as if building a defence. 'Are you and your husband going to the Neighbourhood Watch meeting at Rose Cottage tonight?'

She couldn't help but notice the cloud that passed across Alice's face at the mention of her husband, and her heart did a little backward flip in her chest.

'Yes – after last night I don't think we'd better miss it! Is the old man next door all right this morning, do you know?'

Liz dropped her eyes lest Alice should be as adept at reading her expression as Liz had been at reading Alice's.

'I saw him over the fence earlier – he seems none the worse for his escapade.'

Alice grinned.

'I am glad. I'm looking forward to meeting him, he seems to be quite a character.'

'Oh, he's certainly that,' Liz murmured.

Alice glanced at her watch and made a face.

'How did it get to be so late! I'd better get my skates on if I'm to get a meal on the table before we go out tonight. Will I see you later?'

She'd said will *I* see you, Liz noticed, not *we*.

'Yes – I'll look out for you,' she promised.

That's it, Elizabeth my girl – set yourself up for another dose of misery, she thought to herself as she watched Alice cross the cul de sac to her own house. But not even cynicism could completely squash her newly raised spirits. Going back inside, she found that, for once, she was actually looking forward to a Watch meeting.

Seven

In the spinney by the river, Scott and Tracy kissed lingeringly under the sheltering canopy of the trees. If Tracy had her way, he would come back to the house with her today, for her entire body quivered with longing. She wanted so much more than the chaste kisses they had shared up to now.

She could, of course, proposition him outright, but she wasn't ready to risk rejection like that, not yet. If he refused and she lost the tentative friendship that they had developed, she didn't think she could bear it. Already she found herself living for these trysts while they trained the little pup that Andy had bought her.

If Andy had noticed a change in her these past few days, Tracy guessed that he would put it down to her delight with Sunny. It wouldn't occur to him to think that she might have met someone. The fact that, for probably the first time since she and Andy had met, she had done something totally independently of her husband added to her sense of illicit pleasure and, though she felt the odd twinge of guilt, Tracy revelled in a growing feeling of strength.

Scott smiled down at her as they broke apart, his eyes

roving her face as if he enjoyed looking at each part of the whole.

'You look lovely without makeup,' he said.

Tracy flushed beetroot and pulled away. It hadn't felt right dolling herself up to the nines, as she did usually, to walk the dog, but she hadn't reckoned on Scott noticing. She began to walk quickly along the path, leaving him behind.

'Hey, what did I say?' he said, catching up with her.

'I don't think it's any of your business whether I wear makeup or not,' she snapped at him, calling Sunny to heel and focusing all her attention on the dog.

Surprise at her vehemence flashed across Scott's eyes and Tracy felt rather foolish, though she continued to glare angrily at him. Andy liked her to wear full makeup at all times and positively disapproved of women who left the house without it in place. Not wearing any, she acknowledged silently, was part of her growing rebellion against Andy, and so Scott's implied criticism – she knew that the compliment was a subtle way of letting her know he disapproved – hurt her.

'Look, I'm sorry if I offended you, Tracy. Sometimes I open my mouth before the brain is engaged. It's a habit of mine that often gets me into trouble.'

Tracy looked up at him and frowned.

'Did you mean it?' she asked, wondering for the first time whether, perhaps, she should actually have taken the compliment at face value.

'Did I mean what?'

'That you liked me without makeup?' she explained patiently.

Scott looked bemused.

'You're a lovely girl, Tracy, whether you've got makeup on or not.'

Tracy smiled. She had to remember that Scott wasn't Andy, there was nothing to suggest that he would employ the same tactics as her husband to put her down.

The more time she spent with Scott, the more she liked him. He seemed to like her too, and like her for herself rather than for the image she might create for him.

'I was wondering,' Scott said a few minutes later, 'do you ever manage to get out in the evenings?'

'Of course!' Tracy laughed lightly at him. 'We're going out tonight in fact.'

'I meant on your own, without your husband,' he said drily.

Tracy grimaced.

'I see.' She thought for a moment. 'I suppose I could . . . why?'

Scott shrugged his shoulders slightly and Tracy sensed that he had to pluck up his courage to ask her.

'I thought that maybe, one night, you and I . . . well, you know. Without the dog as a chaperone,' he added, scowling goodnaturedly at Sunny as he scampered round their feet.

Tracy laughed. She seemed to laugh a lot when she was with Scott, another point in his favour. She couldn't remember a time when she had felt like this with Andy.

'That would be nice,' she said now, her eyes locking with his.

Scott leaned forward and kissed her gently on the lips. It was enough to make her want more, but it seemed that she

was going to have to be content with the odd kiss, at least
for the time being.

'Where are you off to tonight?' he asked her as they
resumed walking.

'Only along the road. There's a Neighbourhood Watch
meeting.'

Scott gave her an odd look.

'Neighbourhood Watch? Have you and your husband
belonged to the Holly Lane group for long?'

'Yes, ever since we first moved in.' Tracy avoided his eye
as she thought of what went on at the monthly meetings.
What would Scott make of *that?* 'It should be quite a lively
meeting tonight!' she said.

'It certainly should,' Scott agreed.

For the rest of the walk he seemed preoccupied and Tracy
was relieved when he reminded her that he'd be waiting for
her at the same time the following Monday, though the
weekend loomed ahead, an interminable two day break.

Sheila could hear Rob whistling as he laid out the drinks for
the evening meeting.

'You sound cheerful,' she commented suspiciously.

'That's because I feel cheerful, my own love,' he replied
facetiously.

Sheila went to pour herself a stiff drink. She didn't trust
Rob in this mood, especially not with all the neighbours due
to arrive any moment. She jumped as the doorbell rang.
Glancing at the clock on the mantelpiece, she saw that it
was eight o'clock on the dot.

'That'll be the new people,' she said to no one in particular as she went to open the door.

Alice and Des stood on the doorstep, each clutching a bottle of wine and sporting nervous smiles. Sheila welcomed them effusively and drew them into the living room.

'Oh,' said Alice, glancing around the empty room in dismay, 'are we the first to arrive?'

'Someone has to be the first, Alice,' Des said with false joviality.

'Absolutely,' Sheila said, coming to his rescue as Alice darted him a stony glance. 'You know what people are like – you say eight o'clock and everybody aims for eight fifteen! Actually, darlings, I'm rather glad you arrived first, it gives us a few minutes to introduce ourselves. I feel dreadful for not coming to welcome you to Holly Lane when you first arrived, but you know how it is – time just runs away with one.'

'It all depends on what "one" is doing, doesn't it? Now, my wife here fancies herself as a latter day Mrs Robinson.'

'Shut up, Rob,' Sheila said through gritted teeth as Rob came to join them. He continued as if she hadn't spoken.

'It keeps her so busy! Oh, don't worry – Des, isn't it? Don't worry Des, you're quite safe. You're far too old for Sheila's very specific tastes!'

Sheila glared at Rob and, turning her back on him, flashed Des and Alice a false smile.

'This, as you've probably gathered, is my husband, Rob. Please don't listen to a word he says – he's become so jaded and dissolute over the years that the only pleasure left to him is in shocking people. Sad, isn't it?'

Rob roared with laughter and fixed drinks for their guests who, by now, were glancing nervously at one another as if they weren't quite sure what they had stepped into.

'What do you do, Rob?' Des asked with forced heartiness.

Rob shrugged his shoulders and, with a look that left Des in no doubt that he considered him about as interesting to talk to as a diseased gnat, replied, 'This and that. Alice,' he said, smiling warmly at her, 'that's a lovely dress – the colour reflects the exact shade of your eyes. Don't you think so, Sheila?'

In response, Sheila rolled her eyes heavenward and went to open the front door with a sense of relief as she heard someone knock. Rob, in this mood, was so unpredictable that she knew that her stomach would be tied in nervous grannyknots by the end of the evening.

Her heart sank as she saw Andy and Tracy. There was an atmosphere between them that even the politest of smiles could not dispel which, on top of Andy's usual irritating adoration of Sheila, was more than she could bear. Showing them through to the living room quickly, she excused herself so that she could get a little air.

Outside, she walked to the end of the drive and glanced down Holly Lane. Numbers one and two had already arrived, but there were still lights burning at numbers four and five. As she watched, she saw Liz lock her front door and run across the road towards her.

'You've left your living room light on, Liz,' Sheila called as she approached.

'Yes. I thought it might be wise, with there being a prowler about. I didn't want the place to look empty, especially now that I'm on my own—' She bit her lip and Sheila tactfully changed the subject.

'You're looking rather lovely tonight,' she commented.

She was too, Sheila noted with some surprise. Normally

Liz ambled over to the meetings in whatever she happened to be wearing, obviously without so much as a glance in the mirror before she left. Tonight, though, she was wearing a pair of apple green jeans which moulded her small, rounded bottom and showed off the slenderness of her waist. Instead of one of the usual T-shirts, which Sheila always privately thought made her look as if she'd come in straight from a day's toil, she wore a crisp white blouse with the last three buttons undone so that the two halves could be tied into a knot, leaving a thin line of tanned midriff bare.

Looking at her, Sheila could have sworn that Liz had flushed at the compliment, but it was too dark to tell for certain.

'Am I the last?' she asked.

'Not quite.' Sheila glanced over to number five where the lights were still blazing in almost every room. She felt Liz stiffen beside her, and she linked arms.

'Come inside,' Sheila said, urging her gently up the path. 'Tracy and Andy are here, and that new couple, Des and . . . Annie?'

'Alice,' Liz corrected her, 'we've already met.'

'Have you? Well then, we'll all have a drink while we wait for JD and . . . and everybody to arrive.'

Sonja watched as Lulu put the finishing touches to her makeup in the dressing table mirror. She looked flawless already in a white dressing gown which set off her tan and her hair set in a mass of soft blonde curls. Like a living Barbie Doll.

No one would guess from looking at her that, mere

minutes before, she had been writhing on the bed in the throes of ecstasy while Sonja pleasured her with her lips and tongue. Or that she and JD had spent the entire afternoon welcoming their new house guest in a most unconventional way. Even now, shifting position slightly where she sat on the edge of the bed, Sonja felt the slight soreness between her legs where JD had used a vibrator on her.

Now Lulu caught Sonja's eye in her dressing table mirror. She smiled knowingly, her gaze roving appreciatively over the other woman's tight, red tube of a dress and her long, bare legs which seemed to go on forever.

'Be a love and see where JD's got to, would you?' she asked.

Sonja wandered downstairs, wondering where JD had hidden himself this past hour or more. In the end, she found him pottering about in his greenhouse. He looked surprised as she greeted him and Sonja realised that he had probably lost all track of time.

'Lulu sent me to find you, JD. It's time to go across the road to the Neighbourhood Watch meeting. You have remembered, haven't you?' she added gently.

'Of course I've remembered!' JD retorted forcefully. 'D'you think I'm a blithering fool?'

'Of course not!' Sonja stepped forward and put her hand on JD's arm, wanting to reassure him. 'I've always had the highest regard for you JD,' she added softly.

JD glanced from Sonja's hand to her face and the fierce scowl slipped from his features.

'Do you know, m'dear, you have the most beautiful eyes.'

Sonja laughed throatily and kissed him on the cheek.

'Really, JD – flattery will get you everywhere!'

He smiled, then his face clouded again and he looked away.

'What is it?'

'I don't want to go to the meeting,' he admitted.

'Why on earth not? You'll be the guest of honour tonight, after what you did.'

JD shook his head.

'They all think I'm an old fool. A joke.'

'No they don't! *I* don't think you're any of those things. I think you were very brave.'

He smiled at her, his pale eyes roving her face appreciatively, much as they would a particularly beautiful painting or other work of art.

'Bless you, Sonja dear,' he said, patting the hand which still rested on his arm. 'You're a gem, and no mistake, bothering with an old man like me.'

On impulse, Sonja leaned forward and pressed her lips against JD's cheek. His skin was dry and papery, but warm under hers and she laid her head on his shoulder for a moment as his arms came about her.

'Come on, you two – Sheila will think we're not coming.'

They sprang apart guiltily as Lulu appeared in the doorway of the greenhouse. Sonja saw that she was looking lovely, as always, in a deep rose pink dress that managed to emphasise her every curve even as it skimmed them, but there was something in Lulu's eyes that made Sonja bite her lip nervously.

JD kissed his wife on the cheek as he passed her and she smiled indulgently at him.

'I thought we'd take a bottle of your whisky with us this

125

evening,' she told him. 'Would you mind fetching it? The good stuff, mind!'

'Understood! Won't be a mo.'

The two women watched JD march briskly across the lawn to the house. Sonja had the strangest feeling that she had been left defenceless without him and the look that Lulu turned on her once he was out of earshot reinforced the fancy.

'Don't you ever, *ever* lay a hand on my husband without my being present again,' she said.

Sonja was taken aback. She wasn't interested in JD, not in that way, and she opened her mouth to explain to Lulu that she had misunderstood what she had seen.

'But—'

'No "buts",' Lulu interrupted her, giving her no chance to explain. 'You accept my rules, or you get out – now. What's it to be?'

Sonja stared at the other woman, a woman whom she had been happy to call her friend and whom she thought felt the same way about her. Lulu looked nothing like the easy going, pleasure loving creature that Sonja knew and liked. There was no gentleness in the steely blue gaze with which she fixed her, and no compromise in her stance.

'It's your house, Lulu,' she replied quietly.

'And my husband. Remember that.'

The two women stared at each other for what seemed like an age to Sonja. Then, with a suddenness that made Sonja blink, Lulu's face softened into its usual expression and she slipped her arm through the crook of Sonja's.

'Come on,' she said, as if there had been no harsh words between them at all. 'This is one Neighbourhood Watch meeting that none of us can afford to miss.'

★ ★ ★

As soon as she settled herself in the Blakes' spacious living room and saw the look on Liz's face as she watched the new woman, Sonja knew that she couldn't rely on Liz having her back. Liz might not know it yet, but she was already well on the way to getting over Sonja's departure.

Sonja supposed she should feel insulted by the fickleness of Liz's emotions, but she was more amused than offended. She would always have a fondness for Liz, and she would be glad to see her happy. Though by the look of this Alice, the road to true love was not going to be a smooth one. There was the husband for a start. Sonja gave Des a speculative glance and was disconcerted when he looked up at the very moment and caught her eye. A spark of interest showed in his eyes and Sonja smiled, filing the information away for future reference.

Rob had arranged for the local community policeman to talk to them on basic home security and the first hour of the meeting was taken up with talk of deadbolts and alarm systems and the importance of Watch schemes such as theirs.

'Above all,' he concluded portentously, 'be on the alert for anything out of the ordinary, anything or anyone who seems out of place. It's better to be safe than sorry.'

The policeman declined a drink, protesting that he was still on duty and taking his leave of them with a smile and an obvious pride in a job well done.

After he had seen him out, Rob returned to a living room full of gloomy neighbours, nobody speaking to anyone else, each wrapped up in his or her own thoughts. When Rob clapped his hands together several people jumped, everyone looked towards him, just as he intended that they should.

'Right – now let's get down to the real business of the evening. Who needs a refill? Alice?'

Alice, who had been staring off into space, gave a visible start at the sound of her name.

'Sorry?' she said, embarrassed to find herself the cynosure of all eyes. She felt Des's exasperated glance and blushed.

'Let me refresh your glass,' Rob said, moving to sit next to her on the sofa.

Everyone began to relax as Sheila passed round trays of canapés and nibbles and the various couples split up and began to mingle. Sonja made a beeline for Liz, who had gone into the kitchen for a glass of water.

'Hi,' she said. 'How are you?'

Liz seemed ill at ease and Sonja realised that her guess that Liz was interested in Alice was spot on.

'I'm fine. And you?'

Sonja shrugged.

'Okay. I don't think the new lodgings are going to work out, though.' She told Liz about the scene with Lulu.

'What are you going to do?'

'Look for a place of my own ASAP, I suppose. Meanwhile, I was thinking that I might be able to do you a little favour – for old times' sake, if you like.'

Liz regarded her wearily.

'What do you mean?'

'Alice Grainger?' She smiled as Liz flushed. 'I thought so! Would it help, do you think, if the husband was . . . occupied for a while this evening?'

'Occupied?' Liz echoed cautiously.

'Mmm. You know. Kept out of the way while you get to know Alice better. Catch my drift?'

Liz shook her head, though she was smiling.

'Sonja, you are totally wicked. You do what you like this evening – I can handle my own affairs, thank you. See you later.'

Sonja watched Liz walk out of the kitchen and decided that her old friend needed help far more than she realised.

In the hallway, Sheila was trying to shake off Andy, who was being more than usually persistent.

'I've told you before, Andrew, I'm not interested,' she said bluntly as he tried to edge his hand up her skirt. He looked crestfallen as she adroitly moved out of his grasp and went to talk to JD McFarlane.

'I thought you were so brave,' he heard her saying, 'the way you stood up to the intruder . . .'

The Colonel preened visibly. Silly old fool, Andy thought irritably. He was lucky he hadn't been shot with his own gun. Stuffing his hands into his trouser pockets, Andy scowled across the room to where his wife was chatting animatedly to Alice Grainger. Tracy had been behaving very oddly since he'd bought her that blasted puppy – she'd actually refused him a quick blowjob before they came out tonight. If she had complied, as she usually did to his every demand, he would be feeling relaxed and sociable. Instead he felt prickly and irritable and it was all Tracy's fault. For God's sake, it wasn't as if he expected much of the woman. All she had to do was keep house and make sure he was comfortable and well attended to. Was that so much for a man to expect?

Rob Blake was sitting on the other side of Alice and looked thoroughly put out that she preferred to talk to Tracy. Andy hid a smile. Served the bastard right – it would do him good not to be in control for a change. On an armchair next to him, Sonja was coming on to Des Grainger, who looked guilty and smug all at once. Lucky bugger – it looked like he was in for a treat tonight.

'All alone, Andy?'

He turned to find Lulu McFarlane standing at his elbow, a small smile playing around her lips. He was tempted, but sex with Lulu always involved letting the old boy watch, and Andy wasn't into putting on a show. Still, she did look rather delicious in that dress . . .

'Excuse me,' Sonja said softly in his ear. Andy turned and saw her leading Des out into the hallway. No one seemed to notice as Sonja and Des slipped away, for at the moment that they crept upstairs, Alice suddenly made a loud exclamation.

'That's it!' she cried. 'I knew something rang a bell when that policeman said about looking out for anything unusual!' She turned to Rob. 'The house next to ours: number three – it's supposed to be empty, isn't it?'

'Yes – the Connor family are abroad at the moment,' Sheila confirmed from across the room.

Alice looked quite excited.

'The other night, when I was getting supper, I could have sworn I heard noises from next door. I looked over the fence in the morning, and I noticed that the caravan is parked right by our house. Supposing someone has broken into the caravan?'

'Are you suggesting that our burglar is living in the

Connors' caravan?' Rob asked drily, scepticism dripping from every word.

Alice coloured.

'Well, I just thought I'd mention it. I suppose it does sound a bit far fetched—'

'Not at all,' Liz came instantly to her defence, glaring at Rob who smiled infuriatingly at her. 'Alice is right to tell us. I think we should check it out.'

'Now?' Sheila asked.

'Why not? While we're all together.'

'I agree,' Tracy piped up. 'If that man is living in the caravan, I for one want him out!'

'Right,' Liz looked around at the assembled neighbours. 'That's Alice and I, Tracy – who else is going to come with us?'

'I'll come,' Sheila replied with a shrug. 'Rob?'

'Very well.' His sigh was heavy as he hauled himself up out of the chair. 'I can't see you four ladies going alone.'

Liz glared at him – four of them together hardly qualified as "alone" – but said nothing. She didn't expect anything more than patronising from men like Rob.

'I think JD had enough excitement last night,' Lulu said authoritatively.

'And I'll man the bar while you've gone, Rob,' Andy said, giving Tracy an indolent look when she frowned at him.

Everyone who had decided to investigate stood up and filed out of the room. Alice paused in the doorway, as if just remembering something.

'Where's Des?' she said, puzzlement in her voice.

'Oh, I expect he'll follow on,' Liz said hastily, aware of Tracy's surprised glance as she hustled Alice out of the door.

Once outside it seemed like a less than sensible idea.

'D'you think maybe we ought to call the police?' Tracy suggested as they walked en masse along the cul de sac.

'Nonsense!' Rob said, giving every impression of enjoying himself. 'What would we say? That we have reason to believe our new neighbour is a cat burglar? If, indeed, he is in the caravan after all. Besides, if he is, one man will be no match for all of us.'

'There's probably no one in there,' Sheila said.

'Maybe I imagined the noises?' Alice suggested, glancing at Liz for reassurance.

'Well, we'll soon find out – here we are,' she replied.

Number three was in darkness as Tracy, Sheila and Alice followed Liz along the driveway, with Rob bringing up the rear. He proved himself to be the better prepared by switching on a torch to light their way and, catching a fleeting glimpse of his expression, Sheila realised that he was genuinely enjoying himself.

The windows to the caravan were covered by a dark material, but as they drew closer it was obvious that there was a chink of light around the edge. Liz turned to the others, her eyes shining in the torchlight.

'What do we do now?' she whispered.

Rob manoeuvred himself to the front and, with a sardonic grin at the assembled neighbours, opened the door to the caravan with a decisive flick of his wrist.

What happened next was probably worthy of a comedy sketch. The four women piled into the tiny caravan and overpowered the man who was sitting on the bed watching television. With a great deal of squealing and shouting, they somehow managed to wrap him in a sheet and, between them, restrain him as he reacted to the assault.

Rob, who had been watching the scene from the doorway, took charge quite effortlessly. He seemed, Sheila noted, quite relaxed, not at all concerned by their discovery.

'Calm down, ladies,' he said, stepping forward. 'Let's see what we have here.'

With one deft tug on the tangled sheet, Rob pulled it away from the man's head whilst at the same time leaving his arms pinned to his sides. One of the women gasped as she recognised him.

'Scott!' Tracy cried, hardly able to believe her own eyes. 'What on earth are you doing here?'

Eight

Scott stared at Tracy, guilt colouring his expression as he realised that the game was up.

'I wanted to tell you, Tracy,' he began, but she backed away from him, her face a mask of hurt and bewilderment.

'Tell me what?' she asked, her voice sounding even higher and breathier than usual, 'that you're the burglar that's been terrorising the Lane?'

Scott's face registered genuine surprise at this and he opened his mouth to protest, only to be beaten to it by Sheila.

'He's no burglar,' she scoffed, cupping his chin in her hand and turning his face towards the light. 'I recognise you – you're the Connors' youngest, right?'

Relief passed across his eyes and he nodded.

'That's right – Scott Connor. I have a key to the main house, but I didn't want anyone to contact my parents and let them know I've come home until I've decided what I'm going to do . . . look, do you think you could untangle me from this sheet and I'll explain everything.'

He was looking directly at Tracy as he spoke, but it was

Liz and Alice, after glancing at the others for their approval, who released him.

'Thank you,' he said, rubbing his arms. 'Tracy?'

She wasn't sure what he was asking her so she simply stared at him, not knowing what to think. Once again it was Sheila who broke the silence.

'Well, since it turns out that we know you, why don't you come along to Rose Cottage and join the party?'

Scott held Tracy's eye as he replied.

'That's very kind of you, Mrs Blake. Perhaps I could come on a little later?'

Sheila thought that she had hidden her disappointment that this promisingly attractive young man had eyes only for Tracy quite well, until she felt Rob's amused glance on her.

'Fine,' she said with a shrug of feigned nonchalance. 'Come on, everybody – the champagne will be growing warm!'

Tracy waited until everyone had piled out before saying, 'I'll be along in a minute too.'

Ignoring the way they all glanced significantly at each other, she closed the caravan door and turned to confront Scott.

'I should have told you everything,' he said, pre-empting her.

'Yes,' she said, 'you should.'

'Thanks for saving me from Sheila Blake – she has a liking for men my age, I've heard.'

'Oh yes – Andy follows her around with his tongue hanging out at every Watch meeting. He doesn't realise that as far as Sheila is concerned, he's well past his sell by date!'

They laughed and the awkwardness between them was dispelled. Scott gazed up at her from the bed and held out his arms.

'Come here,' he said.

Smiling, Tracy sank down on to the bed beside him.

In Rob and Sheila's bedroom at Rose Cottage, Andy watched as Lulu knelt on the carpet in front of him and began to unfasten his trousers. He was conscious of JD sitting in the shadows, but his need was too urgent for him to mind. What did it matter that Lulu was doing this more for the old man's benefit than his? It wasn't JD who was about to feel Lulu's soft, pliable lips opening around the head of his cock . . .

He sighed raggedly as Lulu dispensed with his trousers and drew down his boxer shorts. His cock sprang free, tapping the side of her face before he could pull away.

'Manners!' Lulu remonstrated with mock outrage and Andy shivered.

Her fingers were cool as they enclosed him, her long, redpainted fingernails dangerously close to the vulnerable area of his scrotum as, with her other hand, she pulled his foreskin back to reveal the angry red bulb of his glans.

Andy felt as though he was fit to burst and had to grit his teeth, clenching every muscle in his lower body to stop himself from coming there and then and spoiling everything. Lulu made an approving noise at the back of her throat and dabbed at the leaking slit on the end of his cock with the tantalisingly pointed tip of her tongue. Andy drew in his breath and held it as, slowly, she stretched her lips wide and enclosed him.

He felt as if he had come home as Lulu gradually fed the whole length of him into her hot, hungry mouth. Andy felt the perspiration break out all over his skin as her long fingers slid under his balls and manipulated his testicles before easing into the crease between his buttocks.

Andy liked to think of himself as being highly sexed. Certainly, that side of his marriage was both varied and frequent and he prided himself on being able to bring Tracy to orgasm again and again. But Tracy never afforded him the treatment that Lulu was giving him now, drawing out his pleasure, wanting nothing, it seemed, in return except, perhaps, that she should control the moment of his release.

That condition, if it was one, suited Andy just fine. He was putty in her hands, a melting, malleable mass of nerve endings. Lulu could do anything she liked with him, he would submit without a whimper to her every whim . . .

He groaned as she suddenly allowed him to slip out of her mouth and she rocked back on her heels, looking up at him speculatively. Gazing down at her, he could see his penis, shiny with her saliva, rearing up like an angry red sentinel in front of him. He felt as though it was enormous, glaringly freakish, as if it was perfectly capable of spontaneous combustion if Lulu did not resume her tender ministrations at once.

Lulu was smiling, waiting it seemed, for his reaction.

'What . . .?'

'Lie down on the bed, lover,' she said.

Her voice was low but authoritative, and Andy found himself doing as she instructed before he had time to think about it. The bed dipped under his weight, the slippery satin of the bedspread shockingly cool against the heated skin of his buttocks.

'On your back,' Lulu said as she stood and looked down at him. 'Now,' she said as he complied, 'I'm going to give you a treat I don't give many men. I hope you're not going to disappoint me.'

Andy watched, spellbound, as she performed a slow striptease at the side of the bed. First the dress, which she unbuttoned slowly and peeled apart to reveal a deep-rose silk bra and matching panties, generously trimmed with lace. The panties had suspenders affixed which held up her pale bone-coloured stockings, the tops of which banded the fleshy tops of her thighs, cutting slightly into her skin.

Lulu had drawn the curtains as soon as they had arrived in the bedroom, and the room was lit by a single, pink shaded bedside lamp whose light lent a rosy glow to everything it touched. Lulu's face was partially in shadow, so Andy was not able to read her expression. But her face was no longer important to him as he watched her peel her bra away from the generous white globes of her breasts.

'Christ, you're gorgeous,' he breathed, itching to sit up and bury his face between her breasts. Something in Lulu's expression kept him where he was and he could do nothing but watch helplessly as she continued with the striptease.

Taking her time, eking out every moment of tension, Lulu unclipped each of the suspenders in turn. Lifting one foot on to the bed, she rolled her stocking slowly down her leg before pulling it off her toes and tossing it aside with a flourish which was almost theatrical. She repeated the procedure with the other leg. The smooth, silky skin of her legs was close to his face and Andy turned his face to press his lips against her calf.

Lulu knocked him away lightly by flicking her fingertips against his cheek.

'Wait until you're asked, lover,' she said.

Andy felt hot all over. There was something about the timbre of her voice as she spoke that thrilled him even as it mocked him. It wasn't as if he hadn't made love with Lulu before; he had, on one memorable occasion, had the pleasure of meeting her in the middle of an orgy Rob had organised. But he had never been involved with her one to one like this, discounting the fact that her husband was watching. But then, it was almost irrelevant that JD watched them from the shadows. In a curious way that Andy did not care to think about too deeply, it added to his pleasure, revealing an exhibitionistic streak in him that he had never suspected he possessed.

Lulu was standing now, totally naked in front of him, her pretty face serene, perfectly in control. Though she wasn't much older than his wife, Lulu possessed a quiet maturity that Tracy lacked, a self assurance that sent the blood singing through Andy's veins.

This was what he had been hoping it would be like if he ever got it together with Sheila Blake. This was what he had been hankering for – a woman to take control of him, sexually, to take the responsibility for release away from him.

He looked up at Lulu and, as she smiled knowingly back at him, Andy felt she could read his mind. A strange trembling began deep in the pit of his belly, a fluttering that he had never before associated with sexual desire, though that was undeniably its cause.

'There now,' Lulu said, almost kindly. 'I know what you need. Trust me. Do you trust me, Andrew?' she asked, her head held slightly on one side as she regarded him.

Andy tried to speak, but found that no words emerged. It felt as though his tongue had swollen in his dry mouth and a feeling of such helplessness swept over him that he shivered. Lulu lay the flat of her hand on the taut muscles of his stomach, just above the tip of his penis. Her palm felt cool and soft, both threatening yet comforting, all at once. Confused by his own feelings, Andy merely lay still and stared at her.

He watched as she walked naked around Sheila's bedroom, as if she was looking for something. Something was happening to him that he didn't understand, a kind of shifting, a fine tuning of his responses that had him in a state of breathless anticipation. Lulu picked up a scarf which had been draped over the back of a chair. Andy watched as she advanced, twining the scarf around both her hands, as if planning to strangle him with it.

'What . . . what are you going to do?' he managed to croak.

Lulu smiled the knowing, enigmatic smile that thrilled him, but did not answer his question.

'Roll over, lover,' she whispered instead.

Everything in him felt that he should protest, call a halt to this strange game now, while he still had some control over himself. Yet even as his mind rebelled, he found himself obeying her, rolling on to his stomach like an obedient puppy.

141

'Good boy,' Lulu purred, reinforcing the feeling. 'Hands behind your back now.'

Andy complied and, arranging his hands against the small of his back, Lulu tied his wrists together with the scarf. Turning his head, Andy could just make out the figure of JD sitting in the shadows. The old man was very still, but Andy could sense his tension, his absorption in Andy's experience was so absolute.

Closing his eyes, Andy tested the strength of the knot Lulu had tied around his wrists and realised that she was an expert. He felt utterly helpless, as if a certain sequence of events had been set in motion and he was being swept along by them, incapable of independent action. Shame warred with excitement and he squeezed his eyes tightly closed, burying his face in the pillows to hide his expression.

JD watched Lulu in action and marvelled at her expertise. By God, she was magnificent! She winked at him now as she ran her soft, long fingered hands over Andy's back, sweeping down over his buttocks. With one long fingernail, she lightly traced the crease dividing them and his buttocks clenched by reflex. JD smiled to himself. He wouldn't be able to hang on to *that* particular inhibition for long!

They had discussed playing with Andy before and he had always vetoed the idea. To JD the young salesman appeared far too laddish to be any fun, quite boring in fact, but Lulu had always disagreed. Now it seemed that she had been right, and he wrong. Every line of Andy's body, every harsh breath and shuddering sigh, proved that Lulu had read Andy's character exactly.

JD felt an old, remembered stirring in his loins as Lulu

kneaded the tightly clenched muscles in Andy's rear. Ah, but to be able to swop places! To be young and unsuspecting – what he would give to be in Andy's position now, on the verge of discovering one's true sexual potential . . .

Smiling proudly at his wife, JD made himself more comfortable in the chair and prepared to watch her weave her own particular brand of magic.

Andy gritted his teeth as Lulu's fingers gradually insinuated themselves between his tightly clenched buttocks. He didn't like anyone to touch him there, it made him feel uncomfortable. Lifting his head, he tried to twist round to tell her so, but she leaned close to him, her warm breath tickling at his ear as she spoke.

'Roll over.'

He complied, though not without difficulty, for it was surprising how restricting it was without the use of his hands and arms to assist him. After a great deal of wriggling, he positioned himself so that he was lying face up on the bed, his eyes wide as he waited for Lulu to make the next move.

They widened still farther as he saw that she was touching herself; playing with her nipples so that they stood out like cherry stones before allowing her fingers to drift downwards, towards the thick dark mat of pubic hair which grew in clearly defined whorls on her mons. Andy moistened his dry lips with the tip of his tongue, his eyes following the movement of her fingers as they lingered at the top of the cleft between her labia.

His breath hurt in his chest as she used the first and second fingers of one hand to ease the two halves apart to reveal the deep-pink inner lips. Andy could see that they were swollen, their surface slippery with dew, and this evidence of her arousal fuelled his own so that his cock rose until it was almost vertical.

'Lulu—'

'Hush!' she said, abruptly pulling her fingers away from herself and frowning at him. 'If you speak again without permission I shall have to gag you. Do you understand?'

Andy nodded. He would have agreed to anything if it meant that she would recommence touching herself. Lulu smiled at him and slipped her fingers between her legs again. This time she opened herself wider, so that Andy could see the whole of her vulva and the dark, shadowy entrance to her body.

As he watched, Lulu brought her other hand up to her lips and sucked the tip of her middle finger into her mouth. When she drew it out again, it was shiny with saliva. Holding her labia apart with the fingers of one hand, she ran the finger, slippery with saliva, along the engorged pads of flesh, concentrating on the point at which her labia met.

Andy's eyes widened as she circled her fingertip lightly round and round at the apex and gradually her clitoris appeared, a smooth, shiny bead that tantalised him. As she became increasingly aroused, Lulu bent her knees slightly and thrust out her pelvis, tipping it up so that it was caught in the light of the lamp.

To Andy, lying on the bed, she was all pink, shiny, slippery flesh. Compared to her sex, her breasts and her face were in shadow, her legs wide to reveal the most private part of her, as if in a spotlight. She was so close he could smell the heavy, musky scent of her arousal and his hands pulled against their restraint, longing to reach out and replace her fingers with his. He gave a moan of frustration as he realised that he was held fast, and Lulu sighed.

'Uhh, lover . . . I'm so-o wet! So hot and wet and open . . . can you see how open I am? How ready for you? See my clit? See how it swells and hardens?'

Andy was incapable of speech, he made an incoherent noise at the back of his throat as the sweat broke out over his skin. He had to have her, she couldn't keep him hanging on like this for much longer . . . could she?

'Please . . .?' he whispered, not knowing what it was he pleaded for, only that he had to have *something*.

Lulu made a tutting noise and he remembered what she had said about gagging him if he spoke again without her permission. The idea worried him and he shook his head from side to side in denial as she stopped stroking herself and approached the bed.

'Naughty!' she purred, running her fingertip across his lips.

He could smell and taste the feminine secretions on her fingers and he opened his mouth eagerly under the gentle pressure she applied. Drawing her fingers into his mouth, he sucked greedily on them, revelling in the heavy, sea spray taste of her. Lulu watched him through narrowed eyes.

'Mmm,' she whispered, 'it would be a shame to cover up a mouth this clever.'

Dipping her head, she replaced her fingers with her lips. Cupping his face with a palm on each side, she kissed him deeply, leaving him feeling breathless, eager for more. Lulu's eyes rested on his lips as they broke apart and she ran her thumbpad over the sensitive inner surface of the bottom one.

'Such a lovely mouth . . . There are other ways of keeping you quiet, after all . . .'

Andy did not understand at first what she intended to do. His breath hurt in his chest as Lulu climbed on to the bed and straddled him, one knee on either side of his head. He was staring straight into her sex now. He was surrounded by it, sight, smell, taste: all woman.

Sitting back on his chest, Lulu caressed herself for a few moments, stroking and separating the folds of skin, tapping gently on the nub of her clitoris. She smiled at him, then knelt up, pressing the palms of her hands flat against the wall above the bedhead to balance herself. Looking down at him through the valley of her breasts she gave him his instructions in one word.

'Suck,' she said.

Andy did not have time to react to her forthright demand for Lulu lowered herself down on his face almost at once. Wiggling her hips slightly, Lulu positioned herself so that her labia were spread apart over his mouth, as if they were kissing.

Andy liked licking women. He loved to make them come with his tongue, but he had never had the privilege pressed upon him quite so forcefully. Tentatively, he pushed out his tongue and probed at the little bead which was at the centre of her pleasure.

Lulu moaned and gyrated her hips, encouraging him to be more bold. Her obvious enjoyment soon dispelled any feelings of reluctance on his part and within a few seconds he was licking and sucking for all he was worth. Lulu's juices ran down the sides of his face, sticky and warm and copious as he ran the tip of his tongue along the grooves at either side of her labia and circled the taut skin around the entrance to her vagina.

It was the most curious feeling, trying to pleasure Lulu with his tongue when his hands were tied behind his back. His bondage meant that he had to control everything with his lips and tongue and her dominant position forced him to keep going even when he might have chosen to stop.

Stiffening his tongue, he jabbed it into her vagina, feeling the powerful contractions of her internal muscles around it as she raced towards the peak. Stroking a path back up to her clitoris with his tongue, he could feel the small heart pulsing now as the first tremors of orgasm passed through it, then she was coming, her sex mashing against his nose and mouth, half suffocating him, her juices drowning him as she ground herself against his face.

It was too much for Andy. As Lulu climbed off him, he came with a cry of anguish, his sperm jetting in hot, almost painful bursts from his penis, splattering his belly. The release was bittersweet for, good though it was, he knew deep down that there would be a price to pay for it. It was a few moments before he dared open his eyes to see Lulu's reaction.

She was watching him, a half smile playing around her lips as she saw the struggle going on inside him. And he realised that she was pleased he had disgraced himself, that she relished the opportunity for retribution with which he had inadvertently presented her.

'I'm sorry,' he blurted, unwisely.

Lulu's smile widened.

'Oh dear me,' she said sweetly. 'Now I'm going to have to punish you. You're not going to like that, are you, Andy? Not at first . . .'

She turned away and Andy thought she was going to fetch something to clean the semen from his belly. It felt sticky and cold as it dried and he hoped she would use a warm flannel. His eyes widened in horror as she approached him with another scarf.

'Lulu, I don't think—'

'No, lover, you don't think. Lift up your head for Lulu.'

She tied the gag quickly and effectively, then kissed him through it.

'You look delicious like this,' she told him mischievously. 'So helpless – completely at my mercy! I wish I had a camera . . .'

She giggled at his horrified expression. Turning away from him again, she went to fetch something from the shoulder bag she had brought upstairs with her. It was by JD's feet and, as he turned his head to watch her, Andy saw her lean over to kiss the old man. JD cupped both her breasts in his hands and squeezed and kneaded them for several minutes, his thumbs brushing back and forth across the sensitive tips of her nipples. In spite of his recent climax, Andy felt himself begin to stir again at the sight.

It was some moments before Lulu returned her attention to him, and by that time Andy's hands were suffering from pins and needles. The slight discomfort fled from his mind when he saw what Lulu had in her hand. It was a dildo, long and slender and black with a moulded tip the width of which made his eyes water. As he watched, wide-eyed with a potent mixture of terror and hope, Lulu strapped the dildo round her waist.

The absurdity of the long black penis protruding from Lulu's lush womanly body distracted Andy for a moment from what she intended to do with it. Then she produced a tube of lubricating jelly and realisation dawned.

His mind screamed denial and he shook his head from side to side as Lulu carefully unscrewed the cap. She smiled.

'Roll over, lover – there's no escape.'

Andy lay stubbornly staring at her, but Lulu merely shook her head.

'If I have to move you myself you'll regret it, I promise you. Come on, darling,' she said, her tone became softer, more persuasive. 'You know you're going to enjoy it – once the hurting stops. Look – your body knows what it wants.'

Following her gaze, Andy saw that his cock had sprung to life again and was now standing upright, as hard as it had been before. He closed his eyes to mask his shame and confusion, but he rolled over as he had been told.

'Good boy. Now, up on your knees . . . that's right. Arse nice and high . . .'

Her words affected him as much as any action could have. Andy could have wept with shame, yet he knew that Lulu was right: he wanted this, wanted it so badly that he knew if she stopped now he would crawl on hands and knees and beg her to finish it.

'Spread your knees, let me in,' she whispered.

Lulu's fingers were cool as she slipped them between his legs to caress his scrotum. Spreading his buttocks wide with one hand, she squeezed a line of cold, slippery jelly along the crease of his arse.

Behind the gag, Andy could feel the pressure of a scream building as she worked the jelly into the resistant little hole of his anus. He could feel it slipping up inside him, lubricating him ready for the violation to come.

'You're very tight,' Lulu commented as she worked a finger in up to the knuckle. 'Are you a virgin?'

He nodded and, to his horror, he started to tremble. Lulu seemed delighted.

'Don't worry, lover – the first time is always the worst,' she said throatily, her lips against his ear.

Andy wondered whether that was supposed to be reassuring, but he had no more time to think. He felt the bed dip as Lulu positioned herself behind him and the mock penis knocked against his buttocks.

'Keep it up high for me,' she said authoritatively, and Andy felt himself respond by thrusting his arse high in the air.

His muscles clenched reflexively as Lulu guided the head of the dildo to the intended point of entry, but she merely slapped him, hard, on the rump. Andy was so surprised, he let go, and Lulu took advantage of that split second when his defences were lowered.

There was resistance at first, then the muscles in his sphincter gave far enough to admit the bulbous head of the mock penis. Andy bit on the gag, tears springing to his eyes as Lulu eased the dildo slowly and inexorably along the sheath of his back passage.

A creeping, stinging heat replaced the coolness of the lubricating jelly and, for a moment, Andy thought he would not be able to bear it. Lulu stroked his back and his sides, running her hands soothingly over his buttocks and down his thighs, waiting for him to get used to the powerful sensation. Then, gently at first, she began to move in and out of him.

Slowly, beneath the pain, Andy recognised a new and more pleasurable sensation building. He felt as though he was on fire; his stomach cramped and his breathing became ragged. He groaned with relief as Lulu untied the gag and cast is aside.

'There,' she whispered seductively, 'you like being buggered, don't you, Andy?'

'No!' he whispered, so unconvincingly that Lulu chuckled.

'It's all right,' she said, moving inside him, 'let it go. You can come now, with my blessing.'

As soon as she said the words, Andy felt the seed surge up through his cock and burst out of him.

'Oh my God!' he cried as he collapsed, exhausted, against the pillows. 'Oh my God . . .'

Lulu slipped quietly out of him and leaned over to kiss him on his tear soaked cheek.

'Thank you,' he whispered impulsively.

Lulu smiled and kissed him gently on the lips before going over to join her husband in the corner. Andy watched as the odd couple embraced and Lulu began to put on her clothes.

What had happened in this room had been so disturbing, yet so wonderful, he felt a surge of gratitude towards Lulu which words could not express. In one evening she had managed to completely turn around the way he thought of himself, had shaken up the very foundations of his sexual self. And he knew, without a doubt, that whatever happened once he left this room, nothing would ever be quite the same for him again.

Nine

In the caravan parked in the garden of number three, Scott and Tracy finished the pizza they had had delivered and sat contentedly, arm in arm on the untidy bed.

'The neighbours all thought you must be the burglar,' Tracy told him, snuggling closer.

Scott laughed.

'I bet. What did you all think you were going to do if I was?'

'I thought we did rather well, actually, in the circumstances!'

'It must have put a damper on the Watch meeting.'

Tracy looked at him sideways. How much did Scott know about what went on amongst the Holly Lane Neighbourhood Watch members? For some reason she found herself hoping that he wasn't aware of the real purpose of the group. Her heart sank at his next words.

'My parents would never have anything to do with the neighbours – they're not into that sort of thing at all.'

'Oh? And what about you? What do you think about *that sort of thing?*'

Scott looked her straight in the eye.

'I think that if a couple are happy together, they don't need to play those kind of games. That's another reason why I know that your marriage isn't sound.'

Tracy wanted to take him to task for his arrogance, for his blithe assumption that she wouldn't take offence at his candid approach. But she knew he was right and so she said nothing.

As if he had been waiting for an adverse reaction, when it did not occur Scott reached out for her and pulled her into his arms.

'You're worth so much more than that, Tracy,' he said, his face inches from her own.

Tracy stared into his eyes, moved more than she could believe possible by the sincerity of his words. There was something about the timbre of his voice that told her he did not judge her, and that the feelings she had been developing for him from the moment of their first meeting were returned.

It was a tense moment, a moment when Tracy was oblivious to all but the man against whom she was pressed. Everything about Scott seemed to be brought into sharper focus: the tension in his limbs, the steady beating of his heart in his chest, the quiet self assurance emanating from every pore. For the first time in her life Tracy sensed she had met a man who accepted her exactly as she was, who wanted to make no improvements or alterations, who might even love her just for herself.

With a sigh, she swayed towards him, propelled by an all consuming desire to feel his lips against hers. They were warm and firm, welcoming her first with gentleness, then with increasing passion as the first kernels of desire began to grow.

At first, Tracy held back, waiting for Scott to set the pace. It was only gradually that she realised that she was acting out of habit, and that Scott was doing exactly the same thing, treating her with a courtesy and respect that she did not recognise at first.

'I . . . I'm sorry,' she whispered as she broke away.

Scott looked totally bewildered.

'For what?'

'I didn't mean to throw myself at you like that, I—'

'Tracy, Tracy,' he whispered, over and over, interspersing each incantation with tiny kisses all over her face. 'I *want* you to throw yourself at me!' He pulled back and took her face between his hands. Looking deep into her eyes, he made sure he had her full attention. 'I just want you to be sure,' he said solemnly. 'Absolutely sure.'

Tracy felt a sliding sensation in the pit of her stomach as she reacted to the tone of his voice.

'I am,' she said simply.

Scott's face lit up in a smile that made her stomach turn somersaults, then he began to kiss her again, more urgently this time, his hands stroking her body over the stretchy lycra of her dress, moulding and shaping her figure as if trying to imprint it on his memory.

Tracy clung to him, relishing the warm blossoming of desire in the centre of her, realising with a sense of wonderment that she felt absolutely safe with Scott. It was a miracle to her that she could feel such strength of arousal purely through being near him. She had no need of any gadgets or gizmos or cynical manipulations of her feelings. The fact that Scott wanted her for herself was aphrodisiac enough.

She helped him pull the inadequate tube of material which passed for a dress over her head. He lay her down, almost reverently, on the covers and Tracy bathed in the glow of his admiration as his eyes roved her naked body.

'You're so lovely,' he told her. 'So soft . . .'

Tracy shivered as he ran his hand very lightly over the surface of her skin, tracing the dip of her waist. She was sure that she could feel the tiny hairs stand up in response and she wondered, if his touch made her feel like this, how it would be when he touched her where she could feel herself, even now, melting and growing warm?

She ran her fingers through his hair as he kissed the tip of each breast, so gently. Her nipples sprang to life even at so fleeting a caress and he smiled, clearly delighted with their responsiveness. His tongue felt slightly rough as he twirled it around each tumescent nub in turn, licking and kissing her so thoroughly that Tracy thought she would not be able to bear the pleasure of it.

He stopped for long enough to unbutton his shirt. Tracy watched as he pulled it off to reveal the smooth, firm planes of his chest and back. The muscles of his torso were well defined, though not overdeveloped, and what little hair he had on his body was fine and sparse. His nipples were small brown discs topped by two hard, shiny, brown nuts. Tracy longed to draw each one into her mouth and bite on them.

His jeans went next, and with them the plain black jersey jockey shorts. His penis was long and slender, already erect and Tracy gave in at once to the urge to reach out and stroke it.

'Such soft skin,' she murmured, half to herself. 'Softness covering such hardness . . .'

Lowering himself down on the bed beside her, Scott watched Tracy's face as she caressed him. The electric light in the caravan was dim, yet he could see her quite clearly and his lips traced the outline of her face. Keeping his movements slow and leisurely, Scott stroked the generous swell of her breasts, his palm polishing the puckered flesh at the centre until she sighed raggedly and lifted her face for his kiss.

Tracy felt as though she had died and gone to heaven. Scott seemed to know by instinct exactly how to touch her, not so lightly that it tickled, yet not too firmly so that sensation was crushed either. His penis felt curiously familiar in her hand, as if she had held it before. She was convinced that it would feel just as familiar when it was inside her, and she was keen to test the theory as soon as possible.

Scott was in no hurry. Though his cock responded to her loving caresses, he seemed content to kiss and stroke her, fondling her with a tenderness that served only to add to her excitement. As his fingers edged lower, over the soft swell of her belly and into the crisp tangle of pubic hair on her mons, she held her breath, the anticipation growing to the point where Tracy felt she could not bear it for another moment.

'Oh Scott!' she whispered.

Tiny tremors were already travelling through the sensitive folds of flesh between her legs, simply from the referred stimulation of her mound. Scott's fingers described delicate, ever decreasing circles until, at last, they curled into the warm, moist cleft and found the feminine core of her.

His tongue probed her mouth as his middle finger slipped

157

inside her and Tracy reached up to coil her arms around his neck. She wanted him with a passion that she had never felt before and she pressed her pelvis urgently against his, trying to transmit that need without words.

Recognising the strength of her desire, Scott rolled over so that he was covering her body with his. His skin felt hot, his flesh firm against the softness of hers. She drew her legs up, opening herself, bending her knees so that he could fit together with her, their bodies joining in one long easy movement, as if they had been lovers for years.

They lay together for several moments without moving, their gaze locked. Tracy could see the sense of wonder and joy she was experiencing reflected in Scott's eyes and the realisation that he felt the same way added to her pleasure, magnifying it until she had to deepen his penetration by wrapping her legs around his waist and drawing him towards her.

With a muffled sigh, Scott began to move, with perfect control, sliding in and out of her in a slow, choreographed dance of love. With each inward thrust, the silky, pleated walls of her vagina rippled around him, taking him quickly to the brink. Tracy could see the effort it took him to continue until she caught up with him.

Without the clitoral stimulation she normally needed, all of Tracy's pleasure was focused in the hot, wet well of her body. She could feel a sensation of pressure building inside her, a mounting need for release which, when it came, took her completely by surprise.

It was as if a cork had flown from a bottle, releasing a torrent of bubbles from the neck. Tracy cried out and clung to the breadth of Scott's shoulders as the sensation of climax burst from her, precipitating his own carefully controlled release. She felt the seed flow from his body into hers, mixing with her own secretions to form what felt like a whirlpool of sensation. He clung to her just as she did to him, burying his face in the soft, damp valley between her breasts.

Afterwards, they looked at each other, neither willing nor able to hide the effect their coming together had had on them.

'What happened?' Scott whispered, a look of sheer wonder on his face.

Tracy shook her head, her fingers smoothing his hair back on his forehead absently.

'Maybe that was the difference between making love and merely fucking,' she suggested.

Scott smiled.

'Good,' he said, 'because all I ever want to do with you is make love.'

'Again?' she said, smiling.

Slipping out of her, Scott glanced down at his penis, now limp and satisfied.

'In a few minutes,' he conceded, 'though there are lots of other ways we can try in the meantime, aren't there?'

Tracy grinned and made herself more comfortable on the bed.

'Oh, lots,' she agreed, reaching for him again.

Des Grainger lay back in the foaming bubbles in the Blakes' jacuzzi and felt Sonja's toes play against the side of each thigh. He still couldn't quite believe what was happening to him, though his fear that Alice might start hammering on the bathroom door, demanding to know what was going on, had gradually diminished.

'There's a cloakroom downstairs – no one else will come up here,' Sonja had assured him as she locked the door behind them.

Still dumbstruck by the way she had come on to him, Des had watched, wide eyed, as she performed a slow striptease for him, right down to her underwear.

The frustration of the past few days had surged up in him as her slender, delicate body was exposed and he had fallen on her like a ravaging animal. He shuddered to think now what she must think of him, but at the time he simply hadn't cared.

Sonja certainly hadn't objected as he virtually tore her remaining clothing from her, running his eyes, his hands, his lips all over her. Somewhere in the back of his mind he recognised that she was by far the most exquisite woman he had ever had the good fortune to screw, but at that moment he felt so desperate he had only one goal in mind.

She laughed aloud when he lifted her up against the bathroom wall – a light, carefree sound that had spurred him on. He felt ten feet tall as he lowered her on to the straining rod of his penis like a god as she sighed and gasped with each thrust.

It had felt so good, to have a woman so willing, so free from inhibition. Sonja had given herself so generously, with no thought for her own satisfaction or even her own comfort, and Des had been consumed with gratitude when he finally slipped out of her and lowered her to the ground.

His semen had run down the insides of her thighs, mixed with the viscous dew of her own body, and that was when she had suggested they should take a bath together.

'Won't Sheila and Rob mind?' he had asked her, conscious that he had already taken undue advantage of his new neighbours' hospitality.

Sonja had laughed that lovely light laugh and, without answering his question, switched on the taps.

So, now here he was, up to his neck in churning bubbles, sharing a bath with a beautiful woman. And he felt like a king.

'Can I ask you something?' he said, opening his eyes after a few minutes.

'Fire away.'

'Why me?'

Sonja put her head on one side and regarded him thoughtfully.

'Why not you?' she asked him eventually.

Des shrugged, unsure how to reply. If she hadn't noticed for herself what an ordinary bloke he was, he could hardly point the fact out to her, could he? Yet he was puzzled. Nothing like this had ever happened to him before.

Sonja laughed and edged closer to him, manoeuvring herself on to her hands and knees. Her small pointed breasts, topped with bubbles, hung down, almost touching his chest as she eased herself up his body. Des felt his chest constrict and his cock stirred between his legs.

'There's something you should know about me, darling,' she almost purred. 'You see, I like sex. I'm what you might call a genuine nymphomaniac.' She laughed as Des's eyes widened.

'Well, everybody likes sex, don't they?' he said weakly.

Sonja kissed the corner of his mouth, sending a little

thrill of pleasurable sensation zinging along his lower lip.

'Without meaning to sound conceited, I've never met anyone to match me. I like sex – quickie sex, slow sex, straight sex, kinky sex . . .' she paused, noticing how every time she said the word 'sex' Des shivered involuntarily. 'I like sex with men, sex with women, sex with friends and sex with strangers. Anything, just as long as I get it every day, at least once. I've never found one person who can satisfy me totally.'

It was a barely veiled challenge that Des could not resist. His hands came up to hold her hips and he could feel the bones jutting against the skin as she moved. Even in the water, he could feel the heat of her sex as her legs opened and she straddled him.

'*I* can satisfy you,' he asserted, bringing his knee up to spread her legs wider.

Sonja gave him a small regretful smile.

'No, you can't. But we can have an awful lot of fun while I prove it to you.'

To Des's dismay, she stood up. Rising up above him like a naiad, the water cascaded down her body and dripped onto him. He could see her sex, swollen and red between her legs, as she climbed out of the bath and his cock rose up, its tip breaking the surface of the water. Noticing, Sonja bent to drop a kiss on the end before straightening again.

'Are you in tomorrow?' she asked calmly as she dried herself and began to dress.

'It's Saturday – I'll be home in the morning.'

'Good. I'll call round – say ten o'clock?'

'But Alice—'

Sonja silenced him by leaning over the bath and kissing

him deeply. As her tongue snaked around his mouth, Des knew that he would agree to anything to see her like this again.

'I'll call you tomorrow,' she repeated firmly when she pulled away, 'and you can lick my cunt until it's dry before fucking me from behind. All right?'

'Yes,' Des croaked, struggling manfully with the images she had so shockingly invoked.

Sonja laughed as she went over to the door.

'Don't worry, darling – you'll find a way of getting rid of Alice for an hour or two. Unless, perhaps, she'd like to join us?'

Des felt his jaw drop and he quickly snapped it closed again.

'You must be kidding! No, Alice doesn't like sex very much. She certainly wouldn't be interested in doing it with another woman!' He was surprised how much the idea shocked him.

Sonja gave him a level look and he realised that she didn't believe him.

'I shouldn't be so sure of that,' she said softly. 'See you tomorrow, darling.' She kissed the tips of her fingers and waved them to him, then she slipped through the door.

Des stared after her, not quite knowing what to think. He felt as if she had woven a spell around him, making him behave in ways he wouldn't normally dream of. Bewitched. He grimaced at himself, knowing he was almost looking for a way of exonerating himself, seeking recourse in the age old cry of *I couldn't help myself – she threw herself at me!*

Realising suddenly that the bathroom door was now

unlocked, he hauled himself out of the bath and went to shoot the bolt. Imagining the scene if someone *did* walk in on him, he found a fresh towel and dried himself quickly before dressing and going downstairs.

In the living room, Des felt a pang of disquiet as he saw that Sonja was sitting and talking earnestly with Alice and the woman with short blonde hair whom Alice had befriended earlier – Lisa? No, Liz, that was it. Alice glanced up as he entered the room, but she seemed unconcerned by his absence and continued her conversation without so much as a pause to acknowledge him.

Rob pressed a drink into his hand and led him over to sit by Sheila on the green chintz sofa in the corner.

'You're just in time for the highlight of the evening,' Rob told him.

Smiling weakly at his host, Des noticed that his eyes looked bright, the pupils dilated, and he wondered if he had taken something, or whether he was always this excitable.

'You should have seen Scott Connor's face!' Liz was saying to his left.

'These brave people have been out trying to catch the Holly Lane burglar!' Sonja told him, bringing him up to date with the tale being told.

'Yes – where were you?' Alice asked, frowning.

Des froze, his lips working to form the words that would cover him. Glancing at Sonja, he saw that she wasn't going to be any help at all, she was merely watching him expectantly, as were the other women in the room. Help came from an unexpected source.

'When I walked through the door, I found old Des here

had sniffed out my secret supply of old malt,' Rob said, clapping Des on the shoulder heartily. 'He's a man after my own heart, aren't you?'

Des grinned weakly.

'Well, I—'

'I didn't know you liked whisky, Des,' Alice said, her tone puzzled.

'This is no ordinary whisky, my love – believe me!' Rob said, leaning forward to touch Alice's knee in a pally gesture that made her shudder.

It wasn't that Rob was an unattractive man – far from it. In his late forties he had the kind of dark, Romany looks that always wear well and Alice couldn't quite put her finger on why she didn't like him.

'Andy will vouch for my malt, won't you, Andy?'

Everyone looked towards Andy, who was sitting, slumped in the corner, nursing a glass.

'Eh?' he said, looking around him as if he'd forgotten where he was.

Rob laughed and went to refill his glass. Andy raised it in a salute. He wasn't sure where Tracy had got to, but he sure as hell wasn't looking forward to going home tonight.

'I have to keep this stuff hidden while the old Colonel's here – he's a bit partial.'

'Rob! That's very rude – JD brought a decent bottle with him,' Sheila said tetchily from the corner.

'Where are Lulu and JD?' Sonja asked.

'Lulu took the old boy home to bed,' Rob answered her. 'Shame – I think he would have enjoyed the film.'

'What film?' Sonja and Liz asked in unison.

'Wait and see,' Rob said, waggling his eyebrows at them.

Everyone watched as he went round the room, switching off the lamps before he opened the cabinet which housed a vast television screen. 'I think you'll all enjoy this,' he told them, perching on the arm of the sofa, next to his wife.

Des thought of suggesting that they should leave, but was afraid to draw attention to himself. Andy stared at the screen without really taking it in, his mind filled with images of Lulu and what she had done to him, grappling still with the discovery he had made about himself.

Alice, flanked by Sonja and Liz, sat back, unsuspectingly, watched by Rob. He was looking forward to her reaction. Sheila merely waited, wondering if this film could be the cause of Rob's hyperactivity. Any explanation would be welcome. He was becoming increasingly difficult to live with lately, growing more and more jaded, seeking ever more bizarre thrills.

On first sight, the film was a run of the mill porno movie, shot with a camcorder, though fairly professionally done.

Two women, one young and dark skinned, the other older with long red hair pulled back off her face, walk into an hotel room together. On the bed there are two packages, each marked in black felt pen with a name: Leanne *and* Margaret.

The two women look at each other and the young one giggles, rather nervously. Without speaking, the two women open the boxes marked with their respective names. Leanne, the younger of the two, is dismayed to find she has been left a plain white blouse, navy blue tunic, and ugly thick navy knickers. To complete the ensemble, there are white knee high socks and a pair of black plimsolls.

Margaret, on the other hand, has been left a smart two piece business suit in emerald green, under which she is to wear a traditional set of black lace bra and panties with matching suspender belt and cobweb-fine stockings.

Leanne strips off her jeans and T-shirt. She is wearing a plain, white, no nonsense bra and brief set. As she dresses in the school uniform, she looks bored. Margaret is similarly unmoved as she puts on the suit. The two women have contrasting bodies; the one slender and youthful with flawless black skin, small-breasted and big-bottomed, the other very white, her skin almost translucent, and voluptuous, though none the less attractive for it.

Once they are dressed, they look at each other critically. Margaret adjusts the front of Leanne's blouse, her fingers lingering just long enough to make the nipples harden under the thin polycotton. Leanne smiles and tucks a stray wisp of hair behind Margaret's ear. There is a tenderness, an understanding between them apparent in every glance, every gesture.

The door opens and the two women turn as one. A man enters. He is dressed in black leather, literally from head to toe. Trousers, jacket and a concealing full head mask with holes for his eyes, nostrils and mouth. In his hand, he is holding a short handled whip with a split end, trailing half-a-dozen leather fronds.

Leanne and Margaret glance at each other, then they smile at the new arrival. No one speaks. The man hands over money, which is counted and put away. With a flick of the whip, the man indicates that Margaret is to be first.

She seems nervous as she begins to unbutton the jacket. Rather than taking it off completely, she merely leaves it open as she pulls up her skirt. She gasps audibly as the man unexpectedly passes the whip across the band of white skin *between her stocking tops and her panties. Leanne goes over to her and pulls down her briefs, handing them to the man, who puts them in his pocket.*

Walking over to the bed, Margaret lies down on her back and spreads her legs wide. The camera focuses on the shockingly red flesh of her open sex. She appears to be trembling, reacting to the tension in the room. The man trails the fronts of the whip up the slippery crease of her sex and she trembles even more.

With a flick of his wrist, he whips her lightly on the insides of her thighs, just the exposed fleshy part, until the white skin is criss-crossed with bright pink weals. Margaret is breathing heavily now, though it does not appear to be due to any pain. She almost seems disappointed when she is told to slide to the head of the bed and Leanne is brought to take her place.

The man makes the younger woman lie face down on the bed, her head between Margaret's outspread thighs. She begins to tongue the other woman and the man feigns outrage, lifting her hips high and dragging the navy blue knickers down to her knees. Thus she is trapped in position, bound by the panties at the knees.

As the man begins to whip her upturned buttocks, she burys her head in Margaret's sex. Margaret begins to play with her own breasts, lifting them clear of the bra and pinching the nipples between her fingers.

Leanne's bottom is glowing and the man throws the whip aside in order to stroke it. Margaret comes noisily, and Leanne lifts her head. The man indicates by a stinging slap to her rear that she should stay in position, arse high, and that Margaret should join her.

Now there are two naked bottoms presented to the camera.

The man removes Leanne's panties and instructs her to move her knees apart. Margaret follows suit and the two women kneel on the bed, knees and thighs touching, waiting while the man unzips his trousers.

His cock is long and thick, coming fully erect as he strokes it in front of the camera. Leanne moans as he eases into her, moaning louder when, after less than half-a-dozen strokes, he withdraws, plunging into Margaret, moving back and forth between the two women.

'Jesus Christ, Rob!'

Everyone in the living room was startled as Sheila leapt up from her seat and turned off the television set. Glaring at her husband, she turned to the assembled neighbours.

'Show's over folks – time to go home.'

'Sheila, Sheila – there's no need to be rude to our guests,' Rob said soothingly.

Andy, who, watching the two women, had inevitably been reminded of his own recent position, stood up.

'I'd better get home,' he announced vaguely to the room in question.

'Um, Alice and I will walk across with you,' Des ventured, hardly daring to look at his wife.

As Des suspected, Alice had been shocked to the core by the film, but had remained glued to her seat with a mixture of embarrassment and curiosity. Now she leapt up and went to join her husband.

'Yes, thank you for a lovely evening,' she said insincerely.

Rob and Sheila didn't seem to notice them go. Liz followed them without a word, worried by Alice's reaction and aware that it had fuelled Rob's enjoyment. Sick bastard! Anger burned in her chest on behalf of her friend and she vowed to herself that she would find a way to make him pay for embarrassing Alice.

'Oh dear,' Sonja said when she was the only one left, 'it looks like the party really is over. Just as it was getting really interesting too.' Standing, she went over to kiss both Rob and Sheila on the cheek. 'I think you look simply divine in black leather, darling,' she purred in Rob's ear as she left.

'How could you?' Sheila whispered once they were alone.

Bored with the game now his audience had gone, Rob shrugged and turned away.

'Don't make such a fuss,' he said.

'Make a fuss? You show our neighbours a porno film with yourself as the star and you expect me not to make a fuss? What is the matter with you, Rob?'

Rob turned slowly and faced her. At that moment he looked weary, more tired than she had ever seen him, and briefly concern for him overrode her anger. But not for long.

'I don't know how you can treat me so badly, Rob,' she said quietly.

'I can't reverse time, Sheila,' he said, 'I can't grow younger instead of older. I can't be what you want me to be.'

Sheila stared at him, stunned. Her liking for younger men had developed only since Rob had lost interest in her, now here he was trying to make out that her affairs were the cause of the problems between them. She had almost found her tongue sufficiently to take him to task when he suddenly grinned.

'I almost forgot – I brought you back a souvenir,' he told her. And out of his trouser pocket he pulled a pair of panties and put them in Sheila's hand. Looking down, she recognised them as the briefs worn by Margaret, the older woman in the film.

'You bastard!' she screamed, throwing them after him as he strode from the room, chuckling under his breath.

'You bastard,' she repeated quietly once she was alone. 'You've gone too far this time. I'll see that you pay for this.'

Ten

Des watched Alice covertly over the breakfast table. From the dark circles under her eyes he guessed that she had had as troubled a night as he. What would she say if she knew the reason for *his* disquiet?

She looked up at him and he dropped his eyes to his plate, afraid that his guilt was written all over his face. Despite all their marital difficulties, he had never, in the five years they had been married, been unfaithful to Alice. He still wasn't sure what had made Sonja so irresistible to him last night. Maybe it was simply her insistence – he had been flattered that she had chosen him, even after she had confessed to simply wanting sex for its own sake.

'Do you have any plans for today?' he asked Alice after a long uncomfortable silence.

'Yes, as a matter of fact Liz asked me if I'd like to go to visit her supplier with her, but I could always go another time when you're back at work if you'd rather—?'

'No, you go ahead,' Des responded a little too quickly. 'I mean . . . I know you'd enjoy it and I was planning on putting those shelves up in the bathroom that we talked about, so . . . go ahead,' he finished.

Alice smiled at him, though her eyes reflected her puzzlement at his apparent keenness that she should take up Liz's invitation.

'Liz seems very nice,' she said.

'Yes. The rest of the neighbours are all a bit . . . weird, don't you think?'

'Weird? Well, that's one word for it. Last night certainly wasn't quite what I expected.'

'Me neither,' Des replied with feeling. 'What time were you planning to go out?'

'About ten. I should be back in time for lunch.'

'Okay. Leave the breakfast things – I'll see to them.'

Alice's eyebrows rose as she left the table. Coming round to Des she dropped a kiss on the top of his head.

'Such consideration!' she teased. 'What have I done to deserve it?'

She left him alone, battling with his conscience whilst at the same time plotting how he could get word to Sonja.

Andy was waiting for Tracy in the kitchen of number one when she arrived home at ten o'clock.

'Andy! I thought you'd be on the golf course by now!'

Andy looked at her blearily. He'd woken with a first class hangover and hadn't realised Tracy wasn't in bed until after he'd showered.

'I cancelled,' he told her.

'Are you ill?' she asked, never having known him to miss a round.

'Do you care? Where the hell have you been, Tracy?'

He watched as she straightened her shoulders and lifted her chin.

'With a friend,' she replied calmly.

Andy gazed at her, not understanding for a moment what she meant. It wasn't until she spoke again that he realised that he had lost her.

'I'm leaving you, Andy,' she told him. 'I've fallen in love with someone else, someone my own age. I've come back to pack a bag and fetch Sunny.'

Andy had never seen her so self confident, so utterly calm. He was so taken aback that she was half way up the stairs before he reacted.

'What the hell are you talking about?' he blustered, running up the stairs after her. 'You need me – you're nothing without me!'

Tracy turned and looked down at him, the expression in her eyes making him take an involuntary step backwards. Pity, contempt, indifference; three emotions that Andy had never thought to see in Tracy's face.

'I'm sorry, Andy,' she said softly, 'but I've made up my mind. You won't miss me, not really. If you think about it you'll realise, as I have, that you never really saw me as a person at all. You don't love me. Now please don't make a scene.'

Andy watched her, stunned, as she calmly packed a case with the bare essentials before going back downstairs. Going into the kitchen, she greeted Sunny and picked up his lead. Clipping it to his collar, she picked up the little dog, laughing as he licked her face.

As she reached the front door, it was as if a bucket of cold water had been thrown over Andy's head and he suddenly sprang to life.

'If you walk out of that door now, Tracy, there won't be

any way back – you hear? And there won't be any money for you either!'

The look she gave him withered him and he fell silent.

'Goodbye Andy,' she said, and with a toss of her candy-floss curls, she walked through the door, and out of his life.

'Was it awful?' Scott asked her as she arrived back at the caravan with her case.

Tracy considered his question for a moment before shaking her head.

'Sad. Not awful. I only wonder why I didn't do it before. How long shall we stay here?'

Scott grinned at her.

'You're some girl, you know? I thought we'd give it another week while we discuss where we'd like to go.'

'What about Sunny?' They both looked down at the puppy who wagged his tail happily at the sound of his name.

'He could come along while we're in the UK.'

'And if we go abroad?'

'My parents will be back next month – would you be happy to leave him here with them?'

Tracy bent down to fondle the puppy's ears.

'Do they like dogs?' she asked.

'Love them. And you'll love them, Tracy. Once they get over the disappointment of my dropping out of uni they'll be fine.'

Straightening, Tracy grinned.

'OK. So where would you like to go?'

'I thought maybe if we pool our savings, we could travel

as far as they'll take us, then work our way back. What do you think?'

Tracy thought the idea sounded totally crazy and, objectively, she wondered why she wasn't in the least bit anxious. And she knew that with Scott by her side she would travel anywhere.

'It sounds terrific,' she assured him, wrapping her arms around his neck. 'Now, have you any plans for the next few hours?'

He laughed, his hands slipping up under her short jumper to caress the warm bare skin of her back.

'No plans, but plenty of ideas,' he murmured as he lowered her on to the bed.

Des was like a cat on hot coals. Ten o'clock, Sonja had said she would call. Alice left at five to and he was terrified that they would cross in the street outside. Once ten o'clock had come and gone, he began to wonder if he had misunderstood, that Sonja was waiting for him to let her know the coast was clear. But how? He could hardly stroll over to number five and knock on the door. He imagined himself greeting Lulu McFarlane with: 'Hi – could you let Sonja know I'm free for that fuck she promised me now?' and shook his head. Too, too crass.

In the event, Sonja took the matter out of his hands. Alice hadn't been gone more than half-an-hour when she appeared at the back door.

'Were you watching the house or something?' he asked her as he let her in.

'Or something,' she replied flippantly, immediately walking up to him and coiling her lean, lithe body around his. 'I hope you had a good night's sleep, darling! You're going to need all your energy for what I have planned!'

Thinking of his restless night, Des grimaced.

'Would you like a drink?' he asked her.

He'd planned it all – as soon as Alice had left he changed the sheets on the bed they shared and placed one of the bottles of champagne he had bought to celebrate their move into a bucket full of ice on the dressing table. He'd removed all trace of Alice: her hairbrush, her perfume, the little tubes and compacts, everything that would make Sonja feel as though she was intruding in another woman's bedroom.

'All right,' Sonja said, without much enthusiasm.

Des led her by the hand up to the bedroom. He felt hot all over, memories of the night before, vying in his mind with images of what he hoped would happen today, making him crazy. He was already aroused; just the sight of Sonja in her skimpy denim shorts and bright green sun top, her long auburn hair brushed into a smooth, shiny curtain around her bare shoulders, had made him instantly hard. Now his erection pushed uncomfortably against the stiff denim of his fly, every step stimulating him beyond endurance.

Inside the bedroom, Sonja looked around, her vivid green eyes taking in every detail.

'How sweet,' she said, going over to the ice bucket. 'And how decadent – champagne at eleven in the morning?'

Des smiled and took the bottle from her, opening it deftly with barely a 'pop' before filling the two glasses he had laid out earlier.

'I thought it might help the mood,' he said.

Sonja's carefree laughter rang out.

'Darling, I keep telling you – I'm *always* in the mood. You just can't quite bring yourself to believe it, can you? But it was a nice thought,' she added, holding his eye above the rim of her glass as she sipped the bubbly liquid.

Des could not take his eyes from her mouth. Her lips were full and naturally red, her tongue very pink and kitten-ish as she flicked it around the rim of the glass. In the night, he had wondered what had come over him in the Blakes' bathroom; now he knew. Sonja had a presence, an aura, that sent him wild with desire.

'Do you mind if we close the curtains?' she asked him, her voice husky with need. 'Only JD might be training his binoculars on us right now, and we don't want to give him a coronary, do we?'

Des went over to snap the curtains shut with an alacrity that made Sonja smile to herself. She wondered what Des would think if he knew the level of activity JD's heart had been known to stand, but decided against enlightening him. There was something intrinsically straightlaced about Des Grainger which made him all the more interesting. Sonja felt a definite *frisson* at the idea of his finding her so shocking. His innocence was quite a turn on.

'Won't you take off your clothes?' she suggested, moving forward to undo the buttons on his short-sleeved shirt. 'I've been thinking all night about having your naked skin next to mine again . . .'

Des sucked in his stomach as her long, cool fingers opened his shirt and resolved there and then to start work-ing out. He was getting soft around the middle and he hoped she hadn't noticed.

'Me too,' he croaked, failing miserably to attain the

casual, self assured tone he sought.

Sonja stepped back and peeled off the sun top. As Des had suspected, she was naked underneath it, her small, exquisitely shaped breasts rising and falling as she lifted her arms to pull the top over her head. She was wearing the same perfume he remembered from the night before, a musky, woody scent which he had never encountered before, and he breathed in deeply, trying to commit it to memory.

Her shorts eased over her slender hips and slid down her long legs to land in a heap round her ankles. Without taking her eyes from his face, she stepped out of them and kicked them aside. She hadn't been wearing panties and Des found himself face to face with a woman wearing nothing but a pair of strappy medium-heeled sandals.

Suddenly, it felt hard to breathe and he sucked the air in through his teeth as he gazed at her, unsure for a moment what to do next. Sonja took the decision out of his hands. Moving closer to him again, she unbuckled his belt and drew it, tantalisingly slowly, through the belt loops.

Once that was cast aside, she worked the stiff metal button through the buttonhole on his waistband and slowly drew down the zip. Des held his breath now, closing his eyes as she reached into his boxer shorts and drew out his penis.

'Mmm, just look at you!' she said, 'so fat and juicy . . . would you mind terribly, darling, if I had a little taste?'

Managing to match her pseudo-mocking tone, Des shrugged and said, 'Be my guest.'

To his delight, Sonja sank to her knees on the carpet in front of him, his cock still held in her hands. He looked down at the top of her head and further, into the dip between her breasts and beyond, and he knew he would never be able to get enough of this. He was hooked, spoiled forever now for the kind of half measures he had come to expect with Alice.

All these thoughts fled from his mind as Sonja opened her mouth and eased the tip of his cock into her mouth. She made a low, appreciative sound in the back of her throat and fed him in slowly, inch by inch.

Her mouth felt hot and very moist as she held him inside without moving for a few seconds. Des sighed as her tongue flickered along the underside of his cock and she began to move her head back and forth, creating delicious waves of sensation up and down the length of his shaft.

He had never encountered a woman who enjoyed fellatio and he was overwhelmed to realise that, to Sonja, it was a real pleasure. Her enjoyment showed in the way she fondled his testicles, manipulating the hard little balls inside the soft sacs until the skin was stretched taut over the swollen core. She made little muffled noises of ecstasy in the back of her throat and her eyes were closed, her expression one of sheer bliss.

'I can't . . . I'm going to come!' he gasped, trying to pull away.

Sonja held him fast by pressing the palms of her hands against his buttocks and holding him against her face, indicating her willingness to swallow him. It was no good, he couldn't hold out for a moment longer. With a ragged cry, he came, his semen spurting from his cock into Sonja's hot, willing mouth.

Afterwards, she leaned back and licked her lips theatrically.

'Yummy!' she said, grinning up at him.

Des sank down on to his knees, all the strength going out of him. He kissed Sonja all over her face, tasting his own emission on her lips, running his fingers through her hair.

'Thank you,' he whispered.

Sonja raised an eyebrow at him.

'I think, darling, that you have been sadly deprived in the lust department! Come – let's have a little rest before we carry on, shall we?'

Des complied willingly. The way he felt as he lay down beside Sonja on the double bed, he wondered if he would ever be able to maintain an erection again, he felt as if she had drained him dry. Turning his head, he saw that Sonja was looking at him and he sensed that she was merely waiting for him to catch his breath before she would want him to start all over again. And for the first time he wondered if she hadn't been telling the truth after all when she had boasted that she was insatiable.

Number two was probably not the best house for a burglar to visit so soon after the new occupants had moved in, but the intruder had decided that more detailed plans were needed before the Connors' house should be attempted.

The woman had already left, the man was entertaining another neighbour upstairs. The intruder had seen the curtains close to the upstairs window some thirty minutes earlier. Good old Sonja! She was never where she was supposed to be!

It would add to the game to know that Des and Sonja were occupied upstairs while the house was being robbed. It had been a thrill to know that Tracy was downstairs while number one was being done, but to do the business while an illicit liaison was being conducted upstairs had to take the biscuit.

Chuckling, the intruder began to get ready.

Alice and Liz left number four shortly after eleven. Glancing across at her house, Alice saw the bedroom curtains had been closed and she frowned.

'Typical!' she said. 'Looks like Des has gone straight back to bed!' she laughed.

Liz seemed uncomfortable and steered her quickly along the street.

'Why don't we call into the Dog and Duck for a quick drink before we go to the nursery?' she suggested.

She wasn't really one for drinking, but she wanted to keep Alice in her current convivial mood at all costs. If what she thought was going on at number two was true, she was determined that Alice should not be hurt by it. The awful thing was, she had a feeling that this was what Sonja meant when she had said that she wanted to help Liz out regarding her friendship with Alice. Did the girl really think that luring Alice's husband away would make her more susceptible to Liz's dubious charms?

Inside the pub, she sighed heavily. The more time she spent with Alice, the more she recognised in her a kindred spirit, and not just because they shared an interest in horticulture. She was sure that Alice had never had a lesbian experience, but she was equally sure that she would not be averse to it, if the time was right and she allowed herself to let herself go.

If Sonja ruined this for her with her ham fisted manipulations, she felt that she wouldn't be accountable for her actions. Alice was special and this time Liz was determined not to mess up.

They met Sheila at the bar.

'Hello!' she greeted them at once, drawing deeply on the cigarette she had between her fingers. 'You will join me, won't you?'

Though Liz sensed Alice's hesitation, she was concerned to see the lines of strain around Sheila's eyes and she drew up an extra bar stool.

'I'm sorry about last night, Alice,' Sheila said once drinks had been ordered. 'It wasn't a very good introduction to the Neighbourhood Watch group, never mind my husband!'

'It's all right!' Alice replied awkwardly.

'It was a bit . . . unexpected,' Liz conceded, remembering Sheila's reaction when she realised that her own husband was the leading man in the porno movie. Until that moment, if she discounted the role of the man altogether, Liz had found the film quite arousing. Knowing that it was Rob who had been wielding the whip had made her feel quite ill.

'You can say that again! Bastard,' Sheila muttered taking another draught of her lager.

Realising that Sheila was rather the worse for drink, Liz laid her hand on the older woman's shoulder.

'Is everything all right, Sheila?' she asked.

To everyone's horror, Sheila began to cry. Alice fished around in her handbag and passed her a tissue which she used to dab ineffectually at her eyes.

'I'm sorry, I never could stand anyone being kind to me!' she said, attempting to laugh. 'It's just that I'm so worried about Rob. He's always been a little bit off the rails, sexually speaking, but he's got to the point now where the thought of ordinary sex doesn't even give him a hard on.'

'He's just a thrill seeker, Sheila,' Liz said soothingly, thinking of Sonja, 'there are a lot of those around.'

'Oh, I know, but nothing seems to really excite him any more. And he's become so secretive . . . I'm sorry, you don't want to sit here and listen to my woes!'

'We don't mind – what are friends for?' Liz said, attempting to reassure her.

'It's time I was getting back. I wish I swung your way, Liz – you're such a sweet person! I think we'd be good together.' Sheila kissed Liz gently on the cheek and slid off her bar stool. Smiling at Alice, she left them, oblivious to the effect of her casual remark.

'What did she mean?' Alice asked quietly once they were alone.

'About what?' Liz stalled for time, worried that if Alice found out the truth about her at this early stage of their relationship it might frighten her away.

'About the way you "swing",' Alice persisted.

Taking a calming breath, Liz turned to Alice and held her gaze.

'I'm a lesbian, Alice. I hope that doesn't shock you too much.'

Alice blinked, then she shook her head.

'Of course not,' she said at once.

'So you still want to come to the nursery with me this afternoon?'

'Of course!' Alice laughed. 'Why wouldn't I?'

Liz relaxed a little.

'No reason,' she said softly, and she smiled, glad now that the subject of her sexuality was out in the open.

Sonja had a bottle of baby oil in the shoulder bag she had brought with her and Des was enjoying rubbing it into her back and shoulders.

'Mmm – you're a natural, Des,' Sonja told him. 'Could you go a bit lower now, and massage my buttocks?'

Des's hand shook as he spilt oil in the palm and warmed it by holding both hands together. Sonja had promised he could take her from behind today and the mere thought of it brought his cock to full hardness again.

Her bottom was pert and firm, the flesh springy under his fingertips as he massaged and kneaded the twin mounds. As he rubbed in the oil, the two halves were dragged open and closed, giving him a tantalising glimpse of the dark cleft between them. He could see the puckered rose of her anus and he wondered if she would let him . . .

'That's good,' she said now. 'Do you think you could raise me up – maybe put some pillows under my stomach?'

Des didn't need asking twice. Bringing two pillows down from the top of the bed, he eased them underneath her. Now her bottom was presented to him in a perfect oval. Her flawless honeyed skin looked soft and infinitely strokable and Des gave in to the urge to run his fingertips over it. The surface of her skin felt like the downy covering of a peach, and as he parted the two halves and feasted his eyes on the perfect succulent crease he felt a tremor run the length of his spine.

186

Resting his palms lightly on each mound, he bent his head and licked a path along the smooth, sensitive membranes. Sonja moaned and thrust her hips back further. Des circled her anus with his tongue, jabbing at the forbidden orifice with the point.

'Oh yes – fuck me in the arse, Des – use the oil.'

Des's hand trembled as he reached for the oil and dripped it into the valley. Sonja wriggled as it stung the sensitive skin and he worked it in to the little hole, all the while struggling to keep his breathing even for fear that he would hyperventilate if he didn't. The excitement was all too much and he could feel his heart pounding in his chest with an almost painful intensity.

Seized by a recklessness he had never felt before, he buried his face in Sonja's bottom, kissing and sucking at her skin until he couldn't bear to wait any longer. There were condoms in the bedside table, since that was what he and Alice always used, and he reached for one now, unrolling it over the sturdy shaft of his cock before kneeling between Sonja's outspread thighs.

The deep-rose purse of her sex hung below the delectable crease of her arse and he fingered it gently, revelling in the slip and slide of his fingertips against her aroused flesh. He would have her here, later, but now he wanted to breach the final taboo.

Sonja made a deep mewling sound at the back of her throat as Des pushed past the first resistant ring of muscle and the vibration caused by the sound transmitted itself through to his own body. The sensation of sliding into the tight, hot sheath was incredible, like nothing he had ever experienced before. Sonja's muscles seemed to clench in protest at the intrusion, squeezing him, bringing him on far too soon.

'Ah – Sonja – yes—' he gasped as the seed pumped out of him and he collapsed over her back.

He could sense her frustration at the speed at which he had come, but at that moment he couldn't care less. His orgasm had drained him, in more ways than one, and once his shrivelled penis slipped out of Sonja's body it was all Des could do to summon the energy to dispose of the condom and flop down on the bed beside her.

'Des . . .?'

'Half-an-hour,' he begged her, his eyes closing. 'Just give me half-an-hour . . .'

The intruder smiled at the scene enacted through the crack in the bedroom door. Sonja looked furious! She was watching Des now as he dozed, her eyes hard, glittering like emeralds as she waited for him to recover.

You'll have to do better than that, sweetheart, the intruder thought, eyeing Des's limp dick. *He's going to need help to get that back up again!*

Moving away soundlessly, the burglar reluctantly gave up on the idea of going through Alice Grainger's underwear drawer. It was obvious that Sonja wasn't going to join Des in the land of Nod and it was far too risky to hang around. It wasn't until the back door was reached that the intruder thought of looking in the washing machine.

Before too long, the contents of the machine were strewn around the floor of the utility room – the pick of Alice's underwear, just asking to be abducted!

Alice and Liz were tired but happy as they arrived back from the nursery in Liz's elderly 2CV. Alice had been delighted to rediscover the joys of gardening and Liz had enjoyed showing her around the nursery. She had even allowed Alice to talk her into spending some of her precious planting budget on some brightly coloured plants for a hanging basket for the front of the house.

'I'll hold you to your promise to help me make this up!' Liz warned her.

'I'm counting on it!' Alice confessed, smiling at Liz happily.

It was so good to have found someone who was on the same wavelength as herself. Alice had always cherished her female friends, but she had never experienced the same sense of *rightness* as she felt in her relationship with Liz. She felt comfortable with her, as if they had known each other for years instead of days.

As they backed into the driveway of number four, Alice glanced across at her own house and frowned.

'Just look at that – the curtains are still closed upstairs! Surely Des can't still be in bed?'

Liz felt her face grow warm and she busied herself with unloading the plants from the boot so that Alice wouldn't notice. She liked Alice and she felt awful that she herself was responsible for what was obviously going on at number two, albeit indirectly. She hoped fervently that Sonja would be long gone by the time Alice went home and that that colourless husband of hers would have the sense to keep his adventure to himself. The last thing she wanted was to see Alice hurt.

'Let's go and put the kettle on – I don't know about you, but I'm gasping!'

Alice smiled at her and nodded, but as she turned to pick her jacket off the back seat, a movement at the side of her house caught her eye.

'Liz – Liz come here!'

Liz picked up on the urgency in Alice's voice and joined her as she ran to the end of the driveway.

'What—?'

'Coming out of my utility room door – look! There he is! Hey, you – stop!'

She began to run across the cul de sac, Liz hard on her heels, overtaking her as they reached the opposite pavement. Liz could see what Alice had seen now – a figure, all in black, running through the back garden, hoisting himself up the fence as they burst through and throwing himself over.

'Stop him!' Alice gasped and Liz pulled herself up by the arms so that she could see over the fence.

She was just in time to see the man – for she was sure it was a man – running through the field towards the footpath which followed the river. On reaching it, he turned left, alongside Andy and Tracy's garden, running towards the main road. Acting on instinct, Liz threw herself over the fence and gave chase.

Liz was fit and it shouldn't have been difficult to at least keep the intruder in sight, but once she had rounded the slight bend at the boundary between the back gardens of number one and Rose Cottage, she was amazed to find that she was nowhere to be seen.

To her right the river was too wide to cross and, besides, the opposite bank led on to wasteground which was fairly open, offering no hiding place. He could have sprinted to

190

the main road, but he hadn't looked that fast and Liz was puzzled. To her left was the wooded section of the Blakes' large back garden and she felt a shiver run down her spine. Could the intruder have vaulted over the Blakes' fence as he had the Graingers', and be hiding even now just on the other side?

Climbing up, Liz ran her eyes slowly around the trees. It was no good; there were any number of places where a determined burglar could hide.

'Liz!'

She turned as she heard Alice calling her from the opposite end of the path. Jumping down from the fence, she ran to meet her.

'Did you see anyone come out of the path?' she asked.

'No,' Alice gasped, out of breath, 'did you see him?'

'I think he might have gone into the Blakes' garden. Come on!'

The two women ran back the way Alice had come, along the main road, beside Rose Cottage, and into Holly Lane. By the time they arrived at Sheila's front door, Alice was gasping for air. She had a stitch in her side and her lungs felt as though they would explode. Liz, by contrast, was barely out of breath.

'Liz – Alice! What a lovely surprise!'

'We've seen the intruder, Sheila, coming out of Alice's house. We think he might have come into your garden.'

'What, *now*?' Sheila sounded alarmed. 'Should we call the police?'

'Perhaps we ought to look first,' Alice said, reluctant to jump the gun. After all, no one had seen the intruder climb into the garden at Rose Cottage; they were only speculating.

'We don't even know if anything was taken from my house yet,' she pointed out, itching to get back to see what had happened.

'Come on,' Sheila said decisively, 'we'll look together.'

The garden stretched for a good half acre to the fence at the bottom where Liz thought the intruder might have entered. They went out of the back door and skirted the pool, checking the rear boundary before fanning out, making their way back to the house. As she passed the small summerhouse built beneath the shelter of the trees, Liz paused, feeling the hairs on the back of her neck stand up on end.

'Sheila?' she called softly, beckoning her over. 'What's in here?'

'Oh, that's Rob's pottering shed. He spends a lot of time in there, doing God knows what. You don't think . . .?'

'The intruder could be hiding in there – I can't think how he could have got away.'

Alice joined them and the three women looked at each other, wondering what to do next. The matter was taken out of their hands when the door to the summerhouse suddenly opened, making Alice squeal with fright.

'Hello ladies – to what do I owe this unexpected pleasure?'

'Rob!' They all said together.

'I didn't even know you were home,' Sheila said as he locked the door behind him and walked with them back to the house.

'You were busy, so I thought I'd leave you in peace for a while.' He sounded amused.

'Did you see anyone?' Sheila asked him, telling him about

Liz's suspicions that the intruder had escaped through their garden.

'Can't say that I did,' Rob replied.

'What were you doing in there?'

'Just reading the paper. Don't nag, Sheila – I'll end up living in the damn shed otherwise.'

'Well, I'd better get home and see what the damage is,' Alice said.

'I'll come with you,' Liz promised, hanging back a little from the others.

Glancing at the summerhouse, she saw that Rob had secured it with a large new-looking padlock. What on earth did he keep in there that warranted such a level of security? Liz frowned. Sheila had clearly been flabbergasted to find her husband at home and Liz was unconvinced by his explanation. Looking at him now from behind as he walked between Alice and Sheila towards the house, she had a horrible feeling of *deja-vu*. What if . . . but no, it didn't make sense!

'Come on, Liz – I want to get home.'

Alice's voice broke into her thoughts and she hastily pushed speculation aside. Alice was on her way to number two – Liz had far more pressing things to worry about at this moment than the identity of the Holly Lane burglar. Such as stopping Alice from walking in on her husband and Sonja!

The first thing Alice saw when she went through the side door from which she had seen the intruder emerge was her underwear spread all over the floor. She stared at it in horror for a few seconds before quickly gathering it all up and shoving it unceremoniously back into the machine.

That would all have to be washed again!

She couldn't understand how the house could have been burgled while Des was at home. Even if he'd gone back to bed and was asleep, surely something would have disturbed him? Even now there was no response to the sound of the door opening and closing.

Alice glanced into the living room and kitchen to check he wasn't downstairs before making for the bedroom. She was aware that Liz had followed her into the house, but she did not look round as she paused on the landing. There were noises coming from her bedroom, quick, breathy sounds that made her feet slow and the blood pound in her ears.

'Alice—'

She shook off Liz's restraining hand and pushed the bedroom door open. Sonja was lying on the bed, on *her* bed, with her legs folded back so that her toes were pointing to the headboard while Des, *her* husband, pounded into her, his face contorted into a rictus of bliss.

Completely oblivious to everything but his own mounting pleasure, he thrust in and out of Sonja's body with a kind of abandonment, a lack of restraint that Alice had never thought to see him display.

'Oh yes . . . oh sweet heaven . . . take it baby, take it all!' he shouted as he shot his seed.

Alice stood, frozen to the spot, unable to drag her eyes away from the scene. Sonja turned her head and smiled, actually smiled at the two women standing in the doorway.

'Uh . . . oh . . . yes-es!'

Des's triumphant cry filled the room. It wasn't until he was ready to withdraw that he realised that Sonja's interest had wandered. His stomach cramped, his bowels turning to water as he turned his head and saw his wife watching him from the doorway.

'Alice!'

Alice said nothing, just turned her head and fled from the room. Liz looked at the couple on the bed with contempt.

'Is there anything you won't do for a cheap thrill?' she asked Sonja coldly.

The smile slipped from Sonja's face and she looked taken aback.

'I did it for you, Liz, I—'

'No!' Liz cut her off abruptly. 'Don't blame me for this. You did it for yourself, just like you do everything else in your life. What did I ever see in you? You disgust me!'

'Now hang on a minute—'

'Shut up!' both women snapped at Des as he tried to enter the conversation.

'Don't leave like this, Liz,' Sonja pleaded.

But Liz merely shook her head and pulled the door closed behind her. She caught up with Alice in the front driveway.

'Alice, wait!'

Alice turned to her with tears glittering in her light blue eyes.

'How could he? The bastard! How could he?' She began to cry.

Liz hesitated for only a moment before putting her arms around her and holding her close.

'Ssh,' she soothed, 'come on now.'

'What am I going to do?' Alice wailed.

'I'll tell you what you're going to do – you're going to dry your eyes and walk across the road with your head held high. Then we're going to make a cup of tea and take it from there. All right?'

Alice nodded and wiped her eyes on her sleeve.

'Liz?'

'Yes?' she answered as they set off for number four.

'Can I stay with you tonight – just while I work out what I'm going to do?'

Liz disciplined herself to squash the leap of excitement she experienced.

'Of course. You can stay just as long as you need to.'

Alice squeezed her arm.

'Thanks Liz,' she said softly, 'you're a good friend to me.'

From the bedroom of number two, Sonja watched the two women go into number four and knew that, no matter what Liz said now, she would thank her one day for what she had done. And she was glad.

Eleven

Sheila waited until Rob had gone to cash up at the string of antiques shops he owned in the district before calling on each of the neighbours in turn. It was always easier, when she wanted to make plans, to present him with a *fait accompli*.

She went to number five first, to the McFarlane's. JD and Lulu invited her into their elegant living room and listened carefully to what she had to say. When she had finished, Lulu regarded her quizzically.

'But Sheila, surely if you suspect who the thief might be, you should go straight to the police, let them deal with it?'

Sheila's face closed and her lips thinned.

'As I said, I have no proof. Just a suspicion. And I have my own reasons why I don't want the police involved. Of course, if those who have been robbed want to pursue the matter, that's quite understandable. All I'm asking is that you try my way first.'

The McFarlanes looked at each other and Lulu shrugged.

'All right. Tomorrow, you say? What time?'

'Around six. That way it'll still be warm enough to take a

dip in the pool. I'll get Rob to lay on a barbecue – we might as well party while we're trying to catch the crook.' She gave them a small tight smile and said goodbye.

Liz kept Sheila on the doorstep, explaining that Alice was sleeping on the living room couch and she didn't want to disturb her after the upset earlier. She gave Sheila a shrewd look as she listened to what the other woman had to say. So she hadn't been the only one coming to unsavoury conclusions that morning!

'But what do you plan to do if you catch him?' she asked.

'Leave that to me – don't worry, all the neighbours will get the chance to vote on what we should do. Can I count on your support?'

Liz nodded grimly.

'Absolutely. See you tomorrow.'

Leaving number four, Sheila decided to visit the caravan last – she had a special favour she wanted to ask of Scott Connor. At number three, she was taken aback to find Sonja sitting with a stunned looking Des, though that explained why Alice had sought sanctuary with Liz, she supposed.

'So can I rely on you to come tomorrow?' she asked when she had explained everything to them.

Des looked as though he was about to refuse, but Sonja answered for both of them.

'We'll be there. I must say, I'm intrigued. Are you sure you can't tell us any more?'

'Not yet,' Sheila said, standing up. 'All will become clear tomorrow, I promise you.'

She wasn't looking forward to calling on Andy, but number one was the first to be robbed and it was important that all the injured parties should be there at her little get together on Sunday evening.

It was obvious from the moment that Andy opened the door that he hadn't sobered up from the night before.

'The lovely Sheila!' he leered at her. 'To what do I owe this wondrous pleasure?'

'I'd like to invite you and Tracy to a party,' she told him, hoping her distaste for him didn't show on her face.

At the mention of his wife, Andy's expression became ugly.

'Ungrateful little bimbo! She's nothing without me, you know, she can't even decide when to clean her teeth unless I tell her to!'

'I see. Er . . . is Tracy in?'

'No. Aren't you listening to me, you silly bitch? Tracy's gone. Left me.'

Sheila's eyebrows rose, but she said nothing. Andy was obviously in no fit state to answer any questions she might have about her young friend.

'Right,' she said, doing her best to ignore his rudeness. 'Well, darling, do come tomorrow, won't you?' She smiled brightly and made a quick exit.

There was music playing inside the caravan at number three. Sheila knocked on the door, and the music stopped. Scott looked surprised to see her.

'Er – hello, Mrs Blake.'

Sheila ran her eyes approvingly over the lean length of his thighs in his tight-fitting jeans and smiled.

'Call me Sheila, please,' she said. ' "Mrs Blake" makes me feel ancient! Can I come in for a minute, Scott?'

He stepped aside and Sheila went into the caravan.

'Hello, Sheila.'

'Tracy!' Sheila's jaw dropped, then she laughed. 'So this is where you're hiding!'

Glancing from Tracy to Scott and back again, Sheila saw at once how things were and she smiled.

'Well, I'm almost speechless!' she admitted, perching on the edge of the bench in the small kitchen area. 'How long has this been going on?'

'Long enough for us to know it's real,' Tracy said as Scott put his arm around her.

Sheila saw the happiness in her face and felt a pang of envy. When was the last time she had felt like that? Tracy even *looked* different, softer, more relaxed somehow. She wasn't wearing any make up whatsoever and her hair was soft and unstyled. It made her look her age – it had been easy to forget that she was only nineteen.

Giving herself a mental shake, Sheila turned her thoughts to the business in hand.

'I wanted to ask you to a party. My house, tomorrow tea time. The weather forecast is good, so I thought we could have a barbecue, and anyone who'd like to can swim in the pool. What do you think?'

'It's very kind of you to ask us, Mrs . . . Sheila, but—'

'I warn you, I won't take no for an answer. Tracy would like to come, wouldn't you, darling?'

Tracy noticed the faint lines of strain around Sheila's eyes and wondered what was going on. Why was it so important to Sheila that she and Scott should attend her party?

'Of course,' she said softly.

Sheila brightened at once.

'I knew I could count on you! You see, Scott, I need your help.'

Scott's eyebrows rose.

'My help?'

'Yes. You see, if my plan works, tomorrow night we'll catch the burglar and put a stop to his mischief once and for all.'

'I'm all for that!' Scott replied, remembering what Tracy had told him about the break in at her house. 'Go ahead, Sheila – I'm listening.'

At number four, Alice had been disturbed by Sheila's knock on the door. She still felt gritty eyed from the tears she had shed over Des and Sonja, but the shock had begun to wear off and she was angry. Very angry.

'I just can't believe he could do that to me,' she told Liz as she toyed with the plate of vegetable curry she'd had put in front of her. 'I mean, things have never been good between us, but even during the worst times I was never tempted to have an affair.'

'Oh, I wouldn't classify a fling with Sonja as an *affair*,' she said cynically.

'What do you mean?' Alice asked, taking a long draught of her wine.

'It'll just be sex to Sonja.'

Alice made a face.

'Ugh! That makes it worse!'

'Does it?' Liz laughed, refilling both their glasses with the Australian red she'd found at the back of the pantry cupboard.

'Absolutely! Why do people attach so much importance

to sex? I never have understood it. After all, it's really nothing more than a mixing of bodily fluids, is it?'

'Alice!' Liz laughed at the soulless image she had conjured up.

They were sitting in the living room with the curtains closed against the encroaching dusk, twin lamps glowing softly at either side of the sofa. Alice was on the sofa, her tray on her lap, while Liz had her legs curled under on the armchair, balancing her tray precariously on her lap.

Alice looked very pretty in the gentle light of the lamp, despite the slight puffiness around her eyes where she had been crying. Seeing Sonja like that with Des had killed off the residue of feeling Liz had for her, freeing Liz to allow her feelings towards Alice to develop.

From various things Alice had said, coupled with an instinct that rarely let her down, Liz was certain that she was unaware of her true sexual leanings. If only she could lead her gently along the path to enlightenment, Liz was sure that the result would be pleasant for both of them. She didn't want to scare Alice away though, and she resolved to move very, very slowly.

'Do you love Des, Alice?' she asked after a few minutes.

Alice looked uncomfortable.

'I suppose I must do. We've been married for five years.'

'What kind of an answer is that?' Liz asked gently.

'An evasive one!' Alice admitted with a small self-deprecating smile. 'To be honest, I've asked myself that question a lot over the past few months. We've been having marriage guidance, you see, and . . . therapy. Moving here to Holly Lane was supposed to be a new start for us.'

Liz stood up and took Alice's tray off her lap. When she

came back from the kitchen, she sat next to her on the sofa.

'What went wrong? I mean, you must have been happy enough before, when you were first married.'

Alice sighed heavily, a sound that pulled at Liz's heart. She wanted to gather her up in her arms and kiss her face, love her so that she would forget all the sadness and confusion she could see reflected in her eyes, but she dared not. Instead she watched Alice steadily, encouraging her to talk.

'It was all right when I was working. I used to come in at seven and it was nice, you know, to have someone to come home to. But when I think about it, we never really spent much time together. By the time I'd made dinner and cleared away it'd be nine o'clock. A little television and we'd both be ready for bed.'

Liz didn't miss the twist of distaste on Alice's lips as she mentioned bedtime.

'That side of things never was good for you, I take it?'

'No. I'm all right with kissing and . . . touching. It's the rest . . . you know?'

'Well, I'm a bit biased, aren't I? So I'm bound to agree with you on that one.'

'Of course – how silly of me. I'd forgotten.'

Liz felt Alice's curiosity and smiled at her, waiting for the questions to come. It wasn't long before Alice ventured one.

'Have you always known that . . . you know?'

'That I'm a lesbian? I suppose I was always aware that I was different. At school I never could understand what the other girls saw in Spandau Ballet and George Michael!'

Alice smiled.

'Have you never been with a man? I'm sorry – don't answer that. It's none of my business.'

'But you're curious?' Liz asked, resting her fingertips against Alice's arm.

Alice was very aware of the light contact as she nodded.

'I've never been with a man. I like men, some men, as people. But I don't like man as a sexual animal.'

'Animal being the operative word!' Alice said feelingly.

'Would you like more wine? I think there's another bottle in the cupboard.'

'No, I'd better not. I get drunk very easily.'

'Best to keep a cool head,' Liz murmured, earning herself a sharp glance from Alice.

'Isn't it hard for you, Liz, to be what you are?'

'How do you mean?' Liz asked cautiously.

'Well, other people, prejudice in general . . . how do you cope?'

Liz shrugged, but Alice didn't miss the brief wave of sadness that passed across her eyes.

'I live my life the way I choose. It's lonely, sometimes. My father won't have anything to do with me, for example.'

'But that's awful!'

Liz smiled grimly.

'He's a deeply religious man. A minister, no less. Luckily my maternal grandmother stepped in and gave me access to the trust fund left by my mother. That's how I bought this house – my little bit of security. I would have preferred to have found somewhere older, with a bit more character, preferably in the country, but my grandmother asked me to stay close. She's old and frail and she relies on me. Later, when she passes on, I'll sell up and buy my dream home – lots of land and solitude.'

'Like my dad's place. You'd love it there, Liz, and you'd

like my dad. He'd certainly take to you. And he wouldn't care if you were a nun or a brothelkeeper, anyone who loves the land is all right by him! Perhaps . . . would you like to come with me to visit?'

The invitation had been a tentative one, but Alice was surprised by how gratified she felt at Liz's wholehearted response.

'Alice, I'd *love* to!' she said, leaning forward to squeeze her hand.

Liz's hand was warm and soft and Alice imagined that she could feel its imprint on hers long after it had been removed. She caught Liz's eye and, slowly, the smile slid from her face. She could see friendship and affection in the other woman's thoughtful grey eyes, but there was something else there, something deeper which caused a warmth to travel through Alice's body.

She trembled as she recognised desire in Liz's eyes, though she did not recoil. Frowning, Alice tried to conjure up a modicum of disgust, but she could not. Instead, she felt the warmth travel slowly, inexorably, through her body, curling along her limbs, making her feel weak. Trying to mask her confusion, she sought some semblance of normality in conversation.

'All the same,' she said, her voice emerging at a deeper register than was usual, sounding alien even to her ears, 'all the same, you must find life difficult, being different . . .?'

Liz smiled sadly. Her eyes never left Alice's and Alice realised with an instinctive certainty that Liz had guessed exactly how she felt.

'I want the same things as many women want. A home,

security, someone to share my life with.'

'Can that be the same between two women as it can between a man and a woman?' Alice asked.

'Of course. Being gay doesn't mean I'm promiscuous, or incapable of forming a serious bond. I want a life partner – a marriage of sorts. I'll never be content with anything less.'

'What about Sonja? Didn't you feel that with her?'

'I thought I did. I thought I was in love with her, that she could be The One. Even after she left me, I thought I'd lost the love of my life.'

'What made you change your mind?' Alice asked, aware, on some deeper level, that the question was a dangerous one.

Liz regarded her squarely, her eyes glittering in the dim light.

'Then I met you,' she said simply.

Alice felt as though everything had suddenly stopped. The room around her faded; all that she could see was Liz sitting in front of her. More than anything, she could sense Liz's vulnerability and felt a wave of admiration for her, for daring to lay herself open to rejection as she had.

Alice had never felt like this before. She had felt a tremor of arousal, once or twice, in the early days with Des, even on the day they moved into the new house, with the help of the champagne. But she had only ever read about the kind of stomach churning, mouth drying desire which consumed her now. It had never occurred to her that she might desire another woman. She'd never even thought about it. Now, with Liz waiting for her to react, it seemed like the most natural thing in the world. And yet . . .

'I . . . I'm scared, Liz,' she admitted.

'Don't be. There's nothing to be afraid of.'

'I don't know . . . maybe I'm wrong . . .'

Liz leaned forward and touched her, very gently, on the lips.

'Take a chance,' she whispered.

Alice was very conscious of her own heart beating erratically in her chest. There seemed to be a tight band constricting her, making it difficult to breathe. Liz's face was mere inches from her own. She could smell the fresh, outdoors perfume of her skin and see her own reflection in the shiny surface of her eyes. Her lips formed the word that Liz was waiting to hear – *yes*.

Liz's mouth was gentle against hers, tentative at first, as if she was afraid that Alice would take fright and pull away. She tasted of wine and the residue of the meal they had shared and Alice closed her eyes, savouring the new sensation.

It was odd kissing a mouth that was as soft and feminine as her own, but Alice decided that she liked it. It was unthreatening, her tongue did not thrust and conquer, rather it slipped gently between Alice's lips, making her want to open her mouth under the soft pressure. Coaxing rather than demanding, it sampled the sweetness within with a light sweep of the tongue rather than a rasp, and Alice felt a direct reaction deep in her womb.

She was wide-eyed with wonder when they finally broke apart.

'There,' Liz said, her voice soft and musical. 'That wasn't so bad, was it?'

Alice gazed at her with something approaching awe. She wanted to tell her that it was the most moving kiss she had ever shared, that for the first time in her life she hadn't felt herself closing off on the inside, dreading what was to come. Instead of telling, she decided to show Liz how she felt.

Leaning towards her, she touched her lips once more against Liz's, brushing them lightly along the surface so that the slight friction sent a thrill of sensation along all the little nerve endings. Liz sighed and circled her shoulders with her arms.

'Oh, Alice!' she murmured, the break in her voice as she said her name betraying the strength of her emotion. 'Come upstairs with me – let me show you what sex should really be like.'

Alice nodded, beyond self questioning now, swept along by a desire she had never thought to feel. Holding out her hand, she allowed Liz to pull her to her feet. The two women never said a word as they walked slowly from the room, pausing every few steps to kiss or hug, or simply smile at one another. Liz didn't bother to flick the light switch in the hallway, and they walked together up the stairs in almost pitch darkness.

The lamps were already on in the master bedroom, casting a romantic glow across the big double bed which dominated the room. Alice felt her throat grow dry as the sight of it brought home to her exactly what it was she was about to do. Supposing she clammed up with Liz as she did with Des? Maybe she wasn't a lesbian at all, just frigid? Feeling a sudden panic, she turned to Liz.

'Liz, I—'

'Ssh!' Liz silenced her by placing a gentle finger against her lips. 'It'll be all right,' she promised.

To Alice it seemed as though Liz's eyes were all knowing,

all wise, and she felt the panic subside. She trusted Liz, knew instinctively that she wouldn't hurt her, could only bring her joy. Alice smiled.

'I know,' she said.

Liz's hands trembled slightly as she ran her fingertips along the deep V of Alice's blouse. The little hairs on the surface stood on end as Liz passed over them and Alice felt her nipples rise and harden into two painful little nuts as the upper curve of her breast was stroked. She felt fragile, like a reed on a river's edge, blowing in the breeze. If Liz pushed her too hard, went too far, too fast, she would snap, break clean in two, as easily as the reed.

Liz had no intention of rushing. She knew that the longer she kept Alice at this pitch of anticipation, the easier it would be to help her make that final leap into the unknown. Glancing at her face, she saw that she looked quite serene, though her half parted lips and rapid breathing betrayed her arousal.

Slowly, Liz dipped her head and pressed her lips gently against the rapid rise and fall of Alice's breasts. Her skin was warm and soft, a fine film of perspiration pushing through her pores, making it moist. Alice didn't move as Liz unfastened the top two buttons of her blouse and flicked her tongue into the dip of her cleavage.

'Your skin tastes good,' she whispered, straightening. 'Touch me, Alice, touch me as I touch you.'

Alice responded to her request by reaching out to fondle the curve of Liz's smaller breasts beneath her T-shirt. Her nipples immediately sprang erect and Liz smiled ruefully.

'Not quite the same in a T-shirt, is it? Let me get rid of it . . .'

She pulled the T-shirt over her head and cast it aside. Now she stood before Alice wearing only a plain white bra and her jeans and socks. Alice ran her eyes covetously over the smooth, tanned skin, noticing Liz's enviably firm muscle tone and the flat, taut plane of her stomach. Tentatively, she reached out and traced the line of her rib cage, her fingers coming to rest on the stiff waistband of her jeans.

Glancing at Liz, she was encouraged by the darkening of her eyes as she watched her, and Alice knew that Liz would allow her to set the pace, to explore this new experience as she chose. Holding her gaze, Alice began to unbutton her own blouse, shrugging it off her shoulders and feeling it fall down her arms. Pulling her wrists free, she allowed the blouse to fall in a heap on the floor, disregarded.

Alice pushed the tip of her tongue through her lips and moistened them. Liz's eyes followed the movement and Alice felt a shiver travel through her. She began to unfasten her jeans. Immediately, Liz mirrored her movements, so that within minutes they stood facing each other, naked save for bras and briefs.

Impatient for the feel of Alice's lips on hers again, Liz stepped forward and took her into her arms. Alice could feel the heat of the other girl's body as they pressed close, their breasts flattening against each other, their stomachs touching. Liz's skin was silky soft, tanned to a light caramel colour, darkening in the places where her skin was exposed to the sun all year round – her forearms, the back of her neck and her face. Her build was slight, but athletic and Alice could feel the strength in her arms as she held her.

Their kisses were more fevered now, the urgency in each

caress mounting, clamouring for expression. Liz unfastened Alice's bra and peeled it away from her breasts.

'Beautiful,' she murmured, stroking the firm globes of
flesh with her fingertips, bringing her out in goosebumps.

'Let me feel your skin next to mine,' Alice blurted, watching with wide eyes as Liz dispensed with the hooks and eyes
that fastened her bra. Her breasts were smaller than Alice's,
perfectly in proportion with the rest of her body.

Tentatively, Alice reached out and covered one breast
with each of her hands. They felt warm and heavy, the crests
pressing against her palms as she circled them. Liz sighed
and Alice felt a deep, atavistic thrill at this evidence that she
could arouse her.

Suddenly, Liz seemed to grow impatient. She crushed
Alice to her, breasts against breasts, and kissed her deeply.

'I can't stand it,' she confessed as they broke apart.
'Please, Alice, please let me love you!'

Alice held her breath as Liz knelt on the floor in front of
her and drew down her panties. She knew that they would
be damp, and she was unembarrassed. She wanted Liz to
know how she felt, aware that that knowledge could only
add to the other woman's pleasure. She watched as Liz
discarded her own remaining underwear.

Once they were both naked, they took a few moments to
simply look at each other, revelling in the similarities and
differences in their two bodies. After a while, Liz took
Alice's hand and led her over to the bed. They sat down, and
Liz bent her head to take one tumescent nipple between her
lips. Alice gasped as she felt an answering tug deep in her
womb and she meshed her fingers in Liz's short, glossy
brown hair, moulding the shape of her skull.

As she turned her attention to her other breast, Liz stroked the gentle curve of her belly, her fingers brushing against her pubic hair, sending little electric thrills of excitement through her. Liz's mouth was warm and wet. With a deep sigh, Alice sank slowly back against the pillows. She felt weak, heavy limbed and almost drowsy as her entire consciousness focused on sensation.

Liz brought her head up and smiled at her, stroking her hair tenderly away from her forehead.

'All right?' she whispered.

'Oh yes!' Alice felt happy tears well up in her eyes and she smiled.

Liz stroked her palm across Alice's shoulder and traced the shape of her arm with her fingertips. Then slowly, methodically, she worked her way down her body, smoothing and polishing the skin with her palm, so that by the time she reached the apex of her thighs, Alice felt totally relaxed.

Taking the time to kiss her again, Liz gradually insinuated her middle finger between Alice's still tightly closed legs. Alice half expected to be gripped by the usual panic. When it did not come, she let out her breath on a long shuddering sigh, and allowed her thighs to roll apart.

Liz stroked tenderly along the sensitive, moisture slick folds of flesh, her touch light, coaxing the response she wanted from her. Alice clung to her afraid, for a moment, of the strength of her reaction. Liz seemed to know exactly how to touch her, how much pressure to apply and how much she could take on this their first encounter.

Though she brought up the moisture from the lips of her vagina with her fingertips, she made no attempt to enter her, concentrating instead on the area around her clitoris. She did not touch it directly at first, merely circling it with her fingertip, and after a few minutes Alice was desperate for her to take more direct action.

She fondled Liz's breasts, closing her eyes as the sensation of impending orgasm began to build at the core of her. Little mewling sounds came from the back of her throat, sounds of need and of pleasure, and she opened her legs wider, bearing down on Liz's skilful fingers in an unconscious expression of need.

Liz's lips were warm against her forehead as she ran her fingertips, oh so lightly, across the supersensitive nub of her clitoris.

'Oh!' Alice cried out. 'Yes – touch me there . . . ahh!'

Liz's fingertip manipulated the small bundle of nerve endings so that Alice was consumed by her mounting climax. Her mouth stretched wide and she drew her knees up to her chest. Liz began to work faster, her fingers slipping against the dew-soaked folds of her labia as Alice moved her head from side to side.

She came, and it was as if someone had flicked a light switch in her mind. *This* was what she had been missing all her life, this was how sex should be. Crying out her lover's name, Alice clung to her, blindly seeking her lips with her own and trying to convey her joy, her gratitude and her love, all in one kiss.

Liz cupped her entire vulva with her hand, as if trying to contain the explosion of sensation which had taken place there. Alice covered her hand with her own and pressed it against her still throbbing flesh.

'Oh Liz!' she whispered when she regained her breath. 'I never dreamed it could be like that! I never knew—'

'I know. Hush now,' Liz soothed her, drawing her into her arms and pulling the duvet up over them. 'We'll sleep a while.'

'But I want to give you the same,' Alice protested, even as she gave in to the fatigue that had overwhelmed her.

'I know,' Liz answered, her lips against her hair, 'and you will. But not now.'

'But . . . what about you?'

Alice felt Liz's lips curve into a smile.

'I'm happy,' she replied softly. 'We've got all the time in the world, Alice – let's not rush things. Sleep now, we can talk and . . . carry on, if you like, later.'

Alice turned her head so that her cheek was resting against Liz's. Never had she felt such a sense of completeness, such a deep and unshakeable contentment. Within minutes she had drifted into a peaceful sleep, secure in the realisation that she had come home.

Twelve

Sheila watched Rob preparing the barbecue for the party from the kitchen window. He looked tanned and fit, the blue of his open-necked, short-sleeved shirt bringing out the blue of his eyes. That was the first thing she had noticed about him when they first met, the colour of his eyes and, more importantly, the hint of danger they contained.

Turning away with a heavy heart, Sheila went upstairs to get ready. What had happened to him these past few years? She had watched him gradually become more and more jaded, seeking new thrills that never satisfied him for long, always restless, looking for more. Moving away from her.

Well, he wasn't going to move any farther, she promised herself grimly. If what she suspected was correct it had to be stopped, now, before anyone really got hurt.

She paused in her excavation of her wardrobe. Could it really be that Rob, in his relentless search for new thrills had turned to house breaking? That *he* was the Holly Lane burglar?

The evidence was all circumstantial, nothing that the

police could act upon if she took it to them. There was his general distraction these past few weeks, the feeling she had gained that he had retreated into a secret world of his own. Though the thought of it sickened her, she guessed he might well have obtained a thrill from systematically robbing all their neighbours.

Sheila selected a supple black leather corset from her extensive collection of fetish wear. This was one of her favourites, bought for her by Rob in the early days of their marriage. It still fitted her as if it had been tailor made, the carefully structured boning moulding her already slender figure into an exaggerated hourglass shape. Checking her appearance in the mirror, she struggled to pull the lace tightly enough at the small of her back. It was impossible to tighten it as far as it would go without assistance, but Sheila did not want Rob to know what she was wearing and so made do with what she could manage by herself.

Even this was enough to push up her breasts into two creamy mounds which spilled over the top of the corset in an overabundance of flesh. The inverted U shape at the crotch framed the neatly trimmed thatch of black hair on her mons, the suspenders dangling in anticipation down the front of her thighs.

Turning slowly, Sheila saw that the generous contours of her buttocks were displayed to their best advantage, the two fleshy globes very white against the black leather, the faded pink stripes shocking still against the whiteness.

Unclipping the suspenders from the corset she put them back into her drawer. She wouldn't be needing stockings tonight. From the back of her wardrobe she pulled out a pair of shiny black PVC boots which reached almost to the top of her thighs. The heels were high and impossibly thin, the toes tapering to dangerous looking points.

Sheila thought of Rob's reaction when he saw what she was wearing and smiled grimly. He mustn't know, not until the right moment. The moment she picked. Therefore she covered up the entire ensemble with a long black evening dress. It was a bit much for an evening barbecue, but most of the neighbours were accustomed to Sheila being over the top. This time, there would be a purpose to it, as they would soon discover.

Reviewing the rest of the 'evidence', such as it was against Rob, Sheila reflected that, with the exception of the Connors' house, Rose Cottage was now the only property which hadn't been burgled. Number three had an extremely complicated alarm system, so she could understand why the burglar had left that one out. But Rose Cottage was only as well protected as the other properties in the street – why had it been spared? Because its owner was the intruder, she told herself. Rob hadn't been at all concerned when they had all piled over to the caravan thinking that the burglar might have been hiding out there. What a laugh he must have had at their expense!

Then there was the fiasco yesterday when Liz had thought the intruder had jumped over their fence. Liz wasn't one for idle fancies: if Liz said she saw something, then she probably did. Rob could easily have changed his clothes in the summer house before popping out, cool as a cucumber, and making out he'd been reading the paper, having decided not to disturb Sheila when he came home. Besides, she'd found the newspaper he read folded by his armchair later that night.

Liz had guessed. Sheila had seen it in her eyes when she went to her house yesterday. Liz would help her, she was sure.

Sheila wondered how the other neighbours would react when they found out. She didn't want to see Rob arrested; quite apart from the ignominy of it all, she didn't think he really deserved that. No, what she had in mind for him would be a far more effective deterrent than a short spell behind bars. All she had to do was persuade the other residents of Holly Lane, especially those who had been robbed, to agree.

Lulu put the finishing touches to her make up and turned to smile at JD.

'Will I do?' she asked him playfully.

'My dear,' he replied, as she knew he would, 'you'd do for a garden party at the palace!'

She smiled at him tenderly.

'Darling JD – you're so good to me,' she said softly.

JD looked startled. It was rare that Lulu verbalised her feelings in such a way and he was touched.

'You are the sun that lights my twilight years,' he told her, going over to raise her hand to his lips. 'The light of my life.' Their eyes held for a moment, then he turned away. 'I must go and find yet another bottle for Blake, I suppose,' he grumbled.

Lulu listened to him walking down the stairs and brought the back of her hand where he had kissed it to her own mouth. She had married JD because he offered her a life of financial ease whilst allowing her to indulge in any sexual adventure she chose. The only proviso was that he should be able to share in her experiences as an observer. The arrangement had suited her very well right from the start, but she was aware that the parameters of their relationship had long since changed. She might have married JD because he was wealthy and easy going – she stayed with him because she had grown to love him.

It was the first time that Lulu had allowed herself to think that simple truth through and she was stunned by it. JD's days of adventuring, sexual or otherwise, were long over, but he still had a quick wit and an appreciation of all that was beautiful. He made her feel . . . *cherished*, yes, that was the word. He cherished her. And in return, Lulu loved and protected him with a ferocity of which she had never dreamed herself capable.

She was worried about this party of Sheila's. The incident when JD had almost shot the intruder had upset him and she had been concerned for him for several days afterwards. Would it be too much for him to come face to face with the culprit tonight?

Lulu worried at her lower lip as she went to join him. Maybe she should call to say they wouldn't be coming. Then she recalled JD's delight at her seduction of Andy and she smiled. JD was hoping for a repeat tonight, she knew, and who was she to say they weren't going to disappoint him? He was upset that Sonja hadn't worked out. She hadn't come back last night at all and Lulu had a feeling that she was busy arranging alternative accommodation for herself. It was probably just as well, she mused, thinking of the scene she had witnessed in the greenhouse between Sonja and JD before the Watch meeting.

She wouldn't cry off from Sheila's barbecue, she'd just

take the precaution of staying close by JD all evening.

Tracy and Scott hauled themselves reluctantly out of bed.

'Do we have to go?' Tracy complained, watching him as he pulled on his clothes.

Scott turned to her and grinned, his eyes roving lazily over her bare breasts.

'We promised Sheila, remember? Besides – don't you want to know who the burglar is?'

Tracy yawned unselfconsciously and stretched.

'Not really,' she said sleepily. She squealed as Scott unexpectedly whipped the covers from her and slapped her lightly on the bare rump. 'Hey!'

'Up with you, lazybones! Don't you want to find out who nicked your knickers?'

He ducked, laughing, as Tracy threw a pillow at him.

'I don't really care any more,' she admitted with a shudder as she pulled on jeans and a silk shirt. 'That belongs to yesterday.'

Scott held her close and kissed her.

'I know,' he said, stroking her hair off her face with tender fingers. 'But sometimes you have to lay the past to rest before you can move on to tomorrow.'

Tracy gazed at him, unafraid to let the love she felt for him show in her eyes.

'How did you get to be so wise?' she asked softly.

Scott shook his head.

'I listened to you,' he said.

Tracy pushed him playfully in the shoulder.

'Let's go then.'

Tracy wasn't the only neighbour who was reluctant to go to Sheila's party. Alice held back, wanting to prolong the period of isolation she had enjoyed with Liz for as long as she possibly could. She was afraid of letting the world at large in on the precious new world she had so recently discovered.

'Come on,' Liz coaxed her. We needn't stay for long if you don't want to.'

'I don't want to see Des. Or Sonja,' Alice admitted.

Liz regarded her levelly.

'We have to face them some time. Will it make any difference to us?'

Alice shook her head.

'No,' she replied firmly, 'I'm staying – provided you still want me, of course?'

'I don't need to answer that, do I?'

'No. We don't have to play games with each other, do we, Liz?'

'Absolutely not.'

Liz smiled at her. She knew how Alice felt. What they had was so new it seemed like tempting fate to put it on public display so soon.

'It doesn't matter what anybody thinks, you know,' she said gently.

'I don't care, deep down. But you'll have to give me time, Liz, before I can be as brave as you.'

Liz nodded, understanding completely. She had known what she was all her adult life. To Alice the knowledge was new and confusing. As their relationship progressed, as Liz was confident it would, Alice would feel more comfortable with it. Liz wasn't naive enough to think they would ever be able to shout it from the roof tops as more conventional lovers did. On the other hand, theirs was not a love to hide away either, and she knew that together they would find a happy medium.

'I wonder what Sheila is planning for tonight?' Alice said as she brushed her hair.

'Whatever it is, I wouldn't like to be in the burglar's shoes.'

'Do you think she really does know who it is?'

'Yes. Which is why we must be there, to make sure that he is properly punished.'

'By the police?'

Liz gave her an enigmatic look.

'As my grandmother said when my father cut me off – there's more than one way to skin a cat.'

'Right,' Alice said slowly. 'We'd better go and . . . see what's going on then!'

Linking arms they left, laughing together.

Des, unlike his wife, wanted to go to Sheila's party with an urgency that bordered on the desperate. Sonja seemed to think that Alice's departure meant that she could move in and she had proceeded to prove to him, quite comprehensively, that he wasn't up to meeting the challenge she'd set him on Friday night.

He hadn't believed her when she'd announced in the Blakes' spa bath that she was a nymphomaniac. Before he'd met Sonja he'd assumed that nymphomania was a condition dreamed up in a psychiatrist's locker room. But now – now he was desperate to get out of the house for a few hours' respite from her demands.

Maybe Alice would be there and he'd be able to talk to her. He'd thought of going over to number four to speak to her, but Sonja had distracted him every time he tried to leave. It was almost as if she didn't *want* him to speak to Alice. Des couldn't understand her – it wasn't as if she was looking for a permanent relationship with him. She'd already made it clear that the very idea was anathema to her.

'Ready, darling?'

Des turned to find her standing in the doorway. She was wearing dark red trousers in a silky material which clung to every line and crease of her body, delineating the shape of her vulva. In spite of himself, Des felt his cock stir in his trousers and he turned away quickly before she saw it and pounced.

'We'd better hurry,' he said, his voice sounding far calmer than he felt, 'we'll be the last to arrive.'

'But the first to come, isn't that so?' Sonja purred, slipping her arms around his waist and covering the soft bulge at his groin. She squeezed gently and Des groaned, almost lunging at the door and hauling them both through it, for fear that if they delayed now they would never get to the party at all.

Andy was the first to arrive at Rose Cottage. Sheila dispatched him smartly into the garden to help Rob with the barbecue. The two men made polite conversation, neither wanting, really, to speak to the other. Moodily, Andy helped himself to a can of beer.

'On a bender?' Rob asked sardonically when Rob downed the contents of the can and picked up another.

'Any objections?' Andy replied belligerently, then, belatedly remembering that it was Rob's beer he was drinking, he made a face. 'Sorry, mate. I suppose you've heard? About Tracy walking out on me?'

'Sheila mentioned it, yes.'

'Well, you know – it's a bit of a bummer.'

'I'll bet. Bit of a goer, your Tracy, isn't she?'

Andy stared at Rob open mouthed. The man was laughing at him and not bothering to hide it either.

'Why, you—'

'Andy! How nice to see you again, darling!'

Andy whirled round at the sound of Lulu's voice, his cheeks flaming with a mixture of anger at Rob and delight at seeing Lulu.

'Hello, Lulu – Colonel.'

'I see you're in charge of the drinks,' JD said, handing him a bottle of claret.

'And you're chef in chief, Rob,' Lulu remarked, running her fingers provocatively up his arm.

Rob smiled at her, leaning forward to greet her with a kiss. Catching sight of Andy's scowling expression, he made more of a meal of it than he had intended and Lulu raised her eyebrows at him.

'Ah – here's the lovely Tracy and her young student friend,' Rob said, catching sight of the new arrivals over Lulu's shoulder. 'What a lovely couple they make!'

Andy's response was swift and dramatic. He virtually wrenched Lulu away from Rob and kissed her soundly, his hands fastened on the delectable curve of her bottom.

'You'll pay for that later, lover,' she whispered as they broke apart.

Andy felt a deep, dark thrill run through him at her words, more powerful than the stab of anger he felt when he saw that Scott Connor's arm was firmly round Tracy's waist.

Des and Sonja arrived next.

'I see Sonja's fixed herself up with new lodgings,' Lulu breathed as she saw the way the other woman was draped around her new conquest. 'She seems to be working her way through Holly Lane house by house – rather like our burglar, wouldn't you say?'

'Lulu!' JD admonished her mildly. 'Don't be bitchy!'

Lulu and Sonja exchanged tight little smiles and it was left to JD to step forward to greet her. Taking her by the hands, he kissed her once on each cheek, standing back to take a good look at her.

'You're glowing, my dear,' he said approvingly, 'what's your secret?'

Sonja laughed and gave them all a twirl.

'Lots of sex – morning, noon and night,' she told them. 'Isn't that right, Des?'

Des looked horrified that she had brought him into the conversation and everybody laughed.

'You're looking a bit green around the gills, old son,' Rob said. 'Is our Sonja proving too much for you?'

'Of course not,' Sonja said, wrapping herself around him again and saving him from having to reply. 'He's just taking a little time to adjust – aren't you, darling?'

Des felt horribly exposed, yet even as she embarrassed him, Sonja was weaving her usual magic. He could feel an erection pressing against the front of his trousers and he groaned inwardly. Would it *never* go down while Sonja was around? As soon as he possibly could he disentangled himself from her and went to talk to Sheila.

'Have you seen Alice?' he asked her urgently.

'Er . . . no,' she replied cautiously, 'but I think she was planning to come this evening.'

Des looked so relieved that Sheila took pity on him and laid her hand on his arm.

'Darling – things have a way of working out for the best,' she told him kindly.

Des looked startled.

'Everything'll be all right once Alice comes home,' he said firmly. 'Once we've sorted out this little . . . *misunderstanding*. He glanced nervously over to where Sonja was flirting with Andy, as if afraid that she might have heard him. She wouldn't take kindly to being described as a *misunderstanding*, of that he was sure.

'Have a drink, darling,' Sheila urged, pushing him gently in the direction of the drinks table.

Alice arrived with Liz some ten minutes later. She looked radiant and Sheila felt a small pang of sympathy for Des. Had he realised yet that Alice wouldn't be coming home after all? Glancing at him, she saw the way his eyes followed his wife as she walked around the garden with her new love, only gradually making her way over to the group of people clustered at one end of the pool.

'I hope you all brought your swimming costumes!' Sheila said loudly.

Scott and Tracy had. They were wearing them under their clothes and, stripping off to cheers from the assembled neighbours, they dived into the clear blue water, closely followed by Lulu. Resplendent in her evening gown, Sheila watched them, a small smile playing around her lips. Everyone was here; the stage was set. All it would take was a word from her and her plan would be set in motion.

'You're looking very lovely tonight, my own one,' Rob said, appearing silently at her side.

Sheila turned to him and smiled widely.

'Why thank you, darling,' she said, her tone matching his for insincerity. 'I just know that this is going to be a very special party.'

She saw the shadow of concern in the back of Rob's eyes and felt a small stab of satisfaction. *That's it, darling – squirm. See how it feels for the boot to be on the other foot!* she thought. She could see from the look on Rob's face that he didn't like being on the receiving end of the kind of mind games he so liked to play with others.

He was too intelligent not to recognise the danger signals, but without some hint of what Sheila was playing at he stood no chance of countering her moves. Raising his glass to her in a small mocking salute, Rob backed away, leaving Sheila feeling triumphant.

'Round one to me,' she whispered, relishing the fact that, so far, only she knew the rules of the game. She'd got him worried, now it was time to put phase two into operation.

Des waited until Liz left Alice alone while she went to refill their glasses before approaching her.

'Alice,' he said, noticing with a pang how she flinched away from him. 'Please, Alice – can't we talk?'

'I can't see that there's anything for either of us to say that can't be said through our lawyers.'

'Lawyers?' Des felt the panic race through him and he gaped at her. 'Alice – surely it doesn't have to come to that? If you'd let me explain—'

'Explain what?' she interrupted, turning on him furiously. 'Explain that you uprooted me from my home, my friends and neighbours, brought me here for a "fresh start" – your words, not mine, I might add – only to allow me to catch you screwing a neighbour days later?'

Des flinched.

'It's not quite like that,' he protested feebly.

'Yes it is. Go away, Des. Sonja's looking for you.'

The expression of near panic on his face as he glanced over to where Sonja was talking to JD would have been comical if it wasn't so tragic.

'Please, Alice, you've got to come home! I don't know what to do – she's insatiable! Alice . . . I feel as if she's eating me up, bit by bit!'

'Then you'll just have to persuade her to spit you out again, won't you?'

'Have a heart, Alice . . .'

Liz joined them, her expression neutral.

'Are you all right?' she asked Alice quietly.

Alice turned to her and smiled, her arm going about the other woman's waist.

'I'm fine.' The smile slipped as she turned back to Des, without taking her arm from around Liz. 'I do have a heart, Des. And it belongs to Liz.'

Des stared at them, realisation slowly dawning. He recalled Sonja saying he shouldn't be so sure when he had said that Alice would never be interested in making it with another woman, and everything clicked into place. Her frigid response to his lovemaking, her inability to enjoy sex with him – why hadn't he realised before which way the wind blew for her? He felt utterly foolish and terribly, terribly let down.

Seeing the realisation dawning on his face, Liz steered Alice away, wanting to shield her from his reaction. Alice allowed herself to be swept away.

'You didn't need to do that,' she said as they stopped by the house. 'But thanks, all the same.'

Liz smiled at her and nodded, knowing how she was feeling without the need for words.

At the side of the pool, Sheila signalled to Scott. He hauled himself out of the water and announced that he was going back to the caravan for a change of clothes. Minutes after leaving, he came running back into the garden, still in his swimming trunks.

'Someone's broken into the house – I think they're still in there!'

'Not the intruder again!' Andy said angrily.

Sheila watched Rob's face. He looked stunned, knowing that what Scott had said couldn't be true. Yet how could he say that without giving himself away? He had no choice but to follow the pack as they all rushed out of the gates to help Scott 'catch' the intruder.

Tracy and Sheila hung behind. As soon as the garden had cleared, Sheila picked up the keys to the summer house which she had found in Rob's study earlier, and the two of them ran to open it.

'Quickly – I can hear them coming back!' Tracy whispered urgently as Sheila struggled with the padlock.

It broke apart just as everyone piled back in to the garden.

'There was no one there,' Alice said, panting as she joined Sheila and Tracy by the summer house.

Rob saw everyone gathering by his shed and pushed his way through.

'What the hell do you think you're doing?' he exploded as he saw the broken padlock in Sheila's hand.

'There wasn't anyone there because the burglar is right here, in this garden,' Sheila told them all.

Throwing back the door to the shed, she saw everyone's jaws drop. Inside was a mini Aladdin's cave.

'That's my clock!' Sonja said, shock making her voice rise.

'And my underwear!' Tracy said in her high, breathy voice.

'And mine,' Lulu said grimly.

Liz recognised a pair of her plain white panties but said nothing. Alice glanced at her, obviously recognising what had been taken the day before from her own house, and Liz gave a little shake of her head. All the neighbours turned accusing eyes on Rob who instinctively began to back away.

'Now, look . . .' he began, holding up his hands.

'Hold him,' Sheila said and Andy and Des each grabbed an arm. For the first time Rob began to look really alarmed and his eyes fell to meet Sheila's.

'You cad, Blake!' JD blustered, his face turning an unhealthy shade of red as he took a step forward.

'It was you all along,' Lulu said, shaking her head in disbelief. 'How could you?'

'I'll call the police, shall I?' Scott said.

There was a general murmur of agreement.

'Wait a minute,' Sheila said, her authoritative tone cutting through the angry mutterings. 'I know that you are all angry and upset, and rightly so. But before you call the police, I'd like you to consider the consequences of your actions.'

She could see the relief in Rob's eyes at her unexpected intervention on his behalf and felt a perverse pleasure in allowing him to think he was saved for a moment longer.

'You're not suggesting we should let him get away with it?' JD said, outraged.

'No, not at all, JD. Quite the contrary, in fact. Think – what will a magistrate give him for a first offence? Nothing that would act as a deterrent, you can be sure.'

'What do you have in mind, Sheila?' Liz asked calmly.

Sheila glanced around at the assembled residents of Holly Lane and saw that she had all their attention. Then she looked straight at Rob, revelling in the apprehension she could see in his eyes. He was completely at her mercy now, and he knew it. A court case would mean certain ruin and, ultimately, an end to the comfortable lifestyle he enjoyed.

'I think that there are far more appropriate ways of teaching him a lesson,' she said, unbuttoning the front of her evening dress to reveal the outfit underneath.

There was a collective gasp as her naked pubis was exposed and she stepped out of the evening dress. From beside the summer house, she produced a bag which she had left there earlier. Inside there was a pair of long black gloves, made of fine rubber. No one spoke as she carefully put them on. She could feel the tension building, drawing them all in, and knew that everyone would go along with her plans.

Holding Rob's gaze, she reached into the bag and took out the second item she had placed in there. It was a whip, long handled and many thonged, which she cracked theatrically against the side of her PVC booted thigh.

'Take him inside,' she said.

Thirteen

'Jesus Christ, Sheila – what the hell do you think you're doing?' Rob hissed as he was frogmarched into the house.

Sheila ignored him, though she recognised the tremor in his voice which was due not to fear, but to excitement. She felt a thrill of pure energy run through her. She was confident that she hadn't misjudged him, not this time.

'Are you sure about this, Sheila?' Liz asked uneasily. The gathering had the air of a lynch mob and she was uncomfortable with the turn of events.

'Don't worry,' Sheila said. 'He'll squeal a lot, but he'll enjoy this – you'll see. Trust me, I know him!'

'Well, if he's going to enjoy it that much, maybe the police would be the better option,' Liz countered drily.

Sheila glanced anxiously at her.

'Please, Liz, darling – for my sake? I promise you Rob won't forget tonight in a hurry.'

Liz realised that Sheila was as afraid of the police becoming involved as Rob and she felt a twinge of sympathy for her. After all, she hadn't done anything wrong and if Rob should be ruined by a court case, Sheila's lifestyle also would go down the tubes.

'All right,' she agreed and was rewarded by a genuine smile from Sheila.

Inside the house, Rob was being stripped of his clothes by the giggling Sonja, Tracy and Lulu. JD sank into an armchair and Andy and Des stood together watching. Andy felt uneasy, Des merely wished he was somewhere else, anywhere but in this place, with these people. On Friday they had seemed exciting and he had been flattered by Sonja's attention. Now he realised he had been merely the nearest available cock and he felt used and degraded. He resolved to slip away, just as soon as he could be sure that he wouldn't be missed.

Alice hung back, glancing uncertainly at Liz.

'What's she going to do?' she whispered.

Liz shrugged.

'I don't know. Would you rather go home?'

Rob swore loudly as the three women finally succeeded in stripping him naked. To Alice's amazement, he was almost fully aroused, his cock standing to attention, the bulbous tip exposed. She had never experienced anything other than straightforward vanilla sex before and she was intrigued.

Catching Liz's eye she made a face.

'Shall we stay for just a little while? We don't have to join in, do we?'

'You don't have to do anything you don't want to do, Alice. We'll stay, if you like. I have to admit, I wouldn't mind seeing this arrogant, misogynistic, little toe rag get his comeuppance.' She grinned and they joined the others in the middle of the living room.

Sheila was magnificent, standing legs akimbo, her fists placed aggressively on her hips, towering over Rob's prone form on her spike-heeled boots. Everyone fell silent as she glared down at him. Even Rob stopped struggling.

'Sheila—' he began, but she cut across him.

'Shut up,' she snapped. Looking around at the assembled neighbours, she addressed them solemnly.

'This, ladies and gentlemen, is my husband. My cross to bear. A lot of you have been asking *why?* I'll tell you why – he broke into your homes for kicks, because he got a buzz out of being there, maybe it made him feel powerful.' She sneered the last word and everyone looked down at Rob, anything but powerful now. And the more Sheila berated him, the more she scorned and humiliated him, the harder his cock grew, until it was standing to attention, at right angles from his body, and rising.

'Think how it must have thrilled his sick little mind to have you all discussing the burglaries with him, never dreaming that you could actually be talking to the intruder himself! I can only apologise for the distress he has caused you all and hope that, by seeing him punished, you will all feel adequately avenged. On your stomach, darling.'

Rob gazed up at her for several frozen seconds. He was staring up into her quim and he felt his balls swell and harden as they filled. Faces pressed around him, staring, eyes no longer hard with anger, but bright with excitement and lust. He felt helpless, vulnerable in a way he had never experienced before. It wasn't an unpleasant feeling and, slowly, he did as he was bid.

'Up on your hands and knees,' Sheila said.

Rob had never heard that note of command in her voice and, to his surprise, it thrilled him. He winced as she flicked the whip against his thigh and obeyed her without further delay. He thought of the sight he presented, waiting meekly for his punishment in the middle of the living room of his home, and knew that his self image was never going to be quite the same again.

He gasped as Sheila cracked the whip across his raised buttocks.

'That's for number five,' she said, dangling the fronds of the whip in front of his face. 'Apologise.'

Rob's mouth and throat felt dry and he found it difficult to form the words. He gasped again as he experienced a second blow.

'I said apologise,' Sheila said, her voice dangerously low.

He raised his head and looked straight at Lulu McFarlane.

'I'm sorry,' he whispered. 'Aah!'

'That's for number four – apologise to Liz and Sonja.'

'I apologise,' he said, responding at once this time.

'Oh, I don't know that an apology is enough,' Sonja cut in. She smiled as everybody looked at her. 'Would you mind, Sheila, if I had him lick me while you whip him? Only it's making me so *wet*, watching him squirm!'

Rob began to tremble as he sensed the *frisson* of excitement that ran around the room. The air was thick with lust and he knew that he was the focus of it. They could do anything to him, anything at all. Sheila had reduced him to nothing more than a plaything, a mindless toy.

He watched as Sonja removed her underwear and sat down on a hardbacked chair. Slowly, she spread her legs, revealing the sensitive red flesh of her vulva. He could see that she was indeed wet, her labia glistening in the soft lighting of the living room.

'Crawl forward,' Sheila demanded, tapping him sharply on the rump with the whip handle.

Rob edged one hand, one knee before the other. He felt like a dog, robbed of all dignity. To his horror, he realised he liked the feeling. He liked the feeling far too much for his peace of mind.

Burying his head between Sonja's legs, he began to tongue her slippery flesh. She tasted sweet, though it was clear that she had recently made love with another man. Her vulva muffled his cries as Sheila whipped him twice more.

'That was for numbers one and two,' she told him.

She sounded breathless, as if administering the punishment had exhausted her. Rob dared not take his face away from between Sonja's legs to look at her. Sonja was close to coming. Her clitoris was like a hard little nut beneath his tongue and he jabbed at it relentlessly with the point, back and forth until she cried out, mashing her sex against his face until he was gasping for breath.

His backside felt as though it was on fire and he cried out with gratitude when someone stroked it with cool hands. No sooner had Sonja vacated the chair in front of him than another open sex came into view.

'My turn,' Lulu said, her voice hard and pitiless.

Rob began the process again, all the while conscious that someone was working soothing ointment into the crease of his behind. *Not that*, he pleaded silently, *anything but that!*

Lulu climaxed with a sigh and climbed off the chair. Now Sheila herself took up position. Rob set to with renewed vigour, eager to convey his gratitude to her for saving him from the wrath of the neighbours. He arched his back as he felt something smooth and round being pressed into the resistant tube of his anus.

'What is it?' he cried, rearing on his knees.

'It's a string of beads,' Sheila told him. 'Each one is bigger than the last. Sonja will feed them into you one by one and you are to take them and hold them in. Do you understand?'

Rob gazed at Sheila with something approaching awe. She must have planned this down to the last detail. He nodded mutely, feeling the perspiration breaking out on his forehead as a second bead was pressed inside his back passage. It gave him the most curious feeling, as if he needed to evacuate his bowels, and he had to clench his buttocks very tightly in order to stop them from slipping straight out again, thus invoking Sheila's wrath.

The third and fourth beads felt uncomfortable rather than painful, giving him a sense of fullness he had never experienced before. The fifth and final bead took some seconds to insert and he sighed, pleased with himself for taking them all.

'Scott and I are going now, Sheila,' he heard Tracy say.

'So soon? Are you satisfied?' Sheila asked.

Tracy laughed softly.

'Certainly. Have fun, Sheila!'

Looking up, he watched as the girl kissed Sheila on both cheeks, completely ignoring him. From the corner of his eye he saw Des Grainger slip quietly away too. Their indifference to him was harder to bear than the way the others were looking at him. At least with those witnessing his humiliation he felt he was achieving something, regaining some modicum of identity in their eyes.

'Now Rob,' Sheila said, demanding his full attention, 'I'm going to ask Liz to fetch a plastic sheet from upstairs, and then do you know what I'm going to do?'

He shook his head, conscious that he was holding his breath. Sheila smiled at him and he fancied there was a cruel twist to her lips.

'Then I'm going to pull these beads out of your arse very slowly.

'No!' he whispered, horrified.

'Yes. And do you know, you're going to like it so much, it's going to make you come, in front of all these people.'

Rob couldn't imagine why Sheila thought that such a thing would turn him on, let alone make him come, and he clenched his mouth into a stubborn line. Sheila saw and smiled grimly at him. Everyone waited while Liz returned with the plastic sheet, then he was made to stand while it was spread out underneath him. Someone indicated that he should kneel down by exerting pressure on the back of his neck and he knelt, looking up at Sheila who was now standing over him, legs akimbo.

'Do you know how it makes a woman feel to have a filthy little pervert like you going through her underwear?' Sheila said, her conversational tone making her words all the more shocking. 'Well – do you?'

'No,' he croaked.

'No, mistress,' she corrected him calmly.

Rob's eyes widened in surprise, but he repeated the words without protest.

'No, mistress,' he said.

'It makes them feel violated, dirty. So I'm going to make you feel dirty, Rob. Dirty and violated. And you're going to spurt your seed all over this nice clean plastic sheet, and everyone here is going to see the snivelling, pathetic creature you already know yourself to be.'

Rob stared up at her, aroused by her words even as he was horrified by them. The tension in the room closed in on him. He could feel the mounting lust as everyone waited. Rob was conscious of Sonja's hands on his hips, holding him steady.

He flinched as the first bead was jerked roughly from his anus. Then the next. The sensation burning, painful – and incredibly exciting. He had never felt so humiliated – all these eyes on his yielding nether passage and his trembling, uncontrollable cock. He sobbed as the last bead was yanked from his body, precipitating his climax.

'Oh God, oh God!' he cried as he came, his semen spattering the plastic sheet spread over the floor.

He hardly noticed the quick, efficient clean up job performed by those around him, he only knew that what he had expected to be a totally humiliating experience had turned into something much more significant. As Sheila climbed down from the chairs, he threw himself at her feet and pressed his lips against her boot.

'Thank you,' he whispered fervently.

Sheila kicked him lightly with the toe of her boot and he began to shake, overtaken by an emotion he couldn't name, let alone control. He only knew that it was good, so good.

'Sit in the corner,' she snapped at him. 'I'll deal with you later.'

Without thinking to question her, Rob slunk away to the corner of the room, hugging the memory of what had just happened to him, close.

Liz looked at Alice and smiled.

'Seen enough?' she asked.

Alice nodded.

'Let's go home.'

They took their leave of Sheila and went, secure in the knowledge that their love was too precious to share. Liz hadn't really expected Alice to join in with the scene at Rose Cottage, as Sonja so willingly had, but she found that she was relieved all the same. Without realising it, she had been setting Alice a test and, although she deplored the idea of it, she was glad that Alice had passed.

'I don't think I'll go to any more Neighbourhood Watch meetings,' she said.

'Me neither!' Alice agreed with feeling, linking her arm through Liz's.

Andy was shaking, half afraid of the strength of his own reaction to what had been done to Rob. God help him, but he had wanted nothing more than to swap places with him.

'Andy?'

He looked up as Lulu appeared at his elbow. She scanned his eyes and he had the feeling that she could read his thoughts.

'Come home with us,' she said smokily. 'Lulu knows what you want.'

He nodded and went like a lamb.

'Would you like to stay the night tonight, Sonja?' Sheila asked when the other girl was the last remaining guest. She had been very helpful, knowing instinctively just what Sheila wanted her to do.

She smiled now and both women looked at Rob, sitting motionless in the corner of the room, an expression of slavish adoration on his face as he looked at his wife.

'Thanks, Sheila, I'd be glad to. I have the feeling that it could be an interesting night.'

Sheila laughed.

'It already has been,' she said, 'but you're right – the night is still young.' Turning to Rob, she beckoned to him with the crook of her finger. A beatific smile came over Rob's face and he leapt to obey her.

Fourteen

Lulu McFarlane found JD standing at the upstairs window with his binoculars. She watched him from the doorway, not wanting to disturb him just yet. He looked so handsome, his bearing still upright and proud, his good bone structure standing him in good stead as the years took their toll. Lulu had seen pictures of him when he was younger, in his prime. He had been an exceptionally attractive man in a very masculine, British sort of way and she could see echoes of that handsome soldier still in the man standing in front of her today.

It was now two weeks since the fateful barbecue party at Rose Cottage, a fortnight that had seen so many changes in the street it was almost as if the residents had played musical houses.

Andy had only just gone home after spending several nights – and days – with Lulu and JD. She had used him to undertake many little jobs around the house that were too much for JD whilst at the same time making full and improper use of his body. She smiled to herself as she reflected that it had been a very useful interlude.

Sensing her standing behind him, JD turned and smiled

at her. Lulu joined him at the window, slipping her arms around his still trim waist.

'What can you see?' she asked him.

JD put the binoculars to his eyes again.

'Well, the Connors are back – Mrs Connor is washing the paintwork at the front of the house and I can see young Tracy's puppy running round her feet.'

Lulu smiled.

'I wonder how Tracy and Scott are getting on.' The young couple had left on their travels days after Scott's parents had come home.

'Famously, no doubt,' JD replied, 'young love and all that!'

'Hmm. Can you see Andy?'

'No, he took himself off to work this morning. Can't go AWOL forever, what?'

Lulu laughed.

'No, he couldn't. Do you miss him, darling? I know you enjoyed having him to stay.'

'I did. But I like having you all to myself again.' He kissed her before turning his attention back to the street.

'Number two is up for sale again. Des Grainger moved out the day after the party, you know. Terrified of Sonja, I don't doubt!' JD tutted loudly. 'These young chaps – I despair! We were made of sterner stuff in my young day!'

Lulu buried her face in his shoulder and giggled.

'Ah, now there's a true love match! Who'd have thought it, eh?'

Looking over JD's shoulder, Lulu saw Liz and Alice draw up in Liz's old car. They'd been away for the best part of the fortnight, in Wales. The McFarlanes watched as they got

244

out of the car and unpacked their suitcases. There was an air of such happiness about them. JD seemed to have forgotten that he and Liz didn't get on, looking kindly on her.

'Good to see her happy again,' he remarked now, and Lulu could only agree with him.

'That just leaves Rob and Sheila,' she said, 'and Sonja, of course.'

'Ah, well that's where you're wrong, my dear – Sonja has moved on again.'

'Really? When?'

'This morning. She gave me a wave, then jumped into a very posh car – a Porsche, no less.'

'Trust Sonja to land on her feet,' Lulu remarked, without acrimony.

'On her back,' JD said, smiling.

'I wonder how she found the time to meet someone new?'

JD laughed. They all knew that Sheila had kept Rob on a tight rein since the party.

'I wonder how long it will before Rob tires of being Sheila's slave?' he mused.

'Do you think he will?'

'Bound to. Chap like that, never could settle.'

Lulu sighed.

'Poor Sheila, I think she rather likes the new submissive Rob.'

JD put down his binoculars and drew Lulu close.

'That just leaves us, m'dear – the odd couple.'

'The odd couple? Is that really how you see us?'

JD shook his head and the expression in his eyes grew serious.

'No, my dear girl, I don't.'

Lulu smiled at him.

'So – everyone else in the street has had their lives turned upside down by Rob Blake. Where does that leave us?'

'Happy?' JD ventured.

'I think so,' Lulu replied softly.

JD kissed her gently on the forehead.

'I think we've had enough excitement for a while, don't you?'

'I certainly do.'

'What would you say to having a quiet time of it for a while, just the two of us. Maybe we could take a holiday? The Caribbean is nice at this time of year . . .'

'That sounds perfect, JD', Lulu replied, and they went downstairs together, the enduring odd couple.

A Message from the Publisher

Headline Liaison is a new concept in erotic fiction: a list of books designed for the reading pleasure of both men and women, to be read alone – or together with your lover. As such, we would be most interested to hear from our readers.

Did you read the book with your partner? Did it fire your imagination? Did it turn you on – or off? Did you like the story, the characters, the setting? What did you think of the cover presentation? In short, what's your opinion? If you care to offer it, please write to:

> The Editor
> Headline Liaison
> 338 Euston Road
> London NW1 3BH

Or maybe you think you could do better if you wrote an erotic novel yourself. We are always on the look-out for new authors. If you'd like to try your hand at writing a book for possible inclusion in the Liaison list, here are our basic guidelines: We are looking for novels of approximately 80,000 words in which the erotic content should aim to please both men and women and should not describe illegal sexual activity (pedophilia, for example). The novel should contain sympathetic and interesting characters, pace, atmosphere and an intriguing plotline.

If you'd like to have a go, please submit to the Editor a sample of at least 10,000 words, clearly typed on one side of the paper only, together with a short resumé of the storyline. Should you wish your material returned to you please include a stamped addressed envelope. If we like it sufficiently, we will offer you a contract for publication.